PUMPKIN SPICED OMEGA

THE HOLLYDALE OMEGAS BOOK 1

SUSI HAWKE

Cover Art Designed by Cosmic Letterz

Cupid always gives you a second chance...

Join my mailing list and get your FREE copy of
Strawberry Spiced Omega
https://dl.bookfunnel.com/io4ia6hgz8

Twitter:
https://twitter.com/SusiHawkeAuthor

Facebook:
https://www.facebook.com/SusiHawkeAuthor

ALSO BY SUSI HAWKE

Northern Lodge Pack Series

Omega Stolen: Book 1

Omega Remembered: Book 2

Omega Healed: Book 3

Omega Shared: Book 4

Omega Matured: Book 5

Omega Accepted: Book 6

Omega Grown: Book 7

Northern Pines Den Series

Alpha's Heart: Book 1

Alpha's Mates: Book 2

Alpha's Strength: Book 3

Alpha's Wolf: Book 4

Alpha's Redemption: Book 5

Alpha's Solstice: Book 6

Blood Legacy Chronicles

Alpha's Dream: Book 1

Omega Found: Book 2

Omega's Destiny: Book 3

Alpha's Dom: Book 4

Alpha's Charm: Book 5

Omega's Mark: Book 6

Alpha's Seal: Book 7

The Hollydale Omegas

Pumpkin Spiced Omega: Book 1

Cinnamon Spiced Omega: Book 2

Peppermint Spiced Omega: Book 3

Champagne Spiced Omega: Book 4

Chocolate Spiced Omega: Book 5

Shamrock Spiced Omega: Book 6

Marshmallow Spiced Omega: Book 7

Three Hearts Collection

(with Harper B. Cole)

The Surrogate Omega: Book 1

The Divorced Omega: Book 2

Waking the Dragons

(with Piper Scott)

Alpha Awakened: Book 1

Alpha Ablaze: Book 2

Alpha Deceived: Book 3

Alpha Victorious: Book 4

Team A.L.P.H.A.

(with Crista Crown)

Grabbed: Book 1

Taken: Book 2

MacIntosh Meadows

The Alpha's Widower: Book 1

The Omega's Dance: Book 2

This is lovingly dedicated to my gurl "A" with lots & lots of huggles and many thanks for all the patient encouragement, sweet friendship, magickal cover skills and most importantly: for being an awesome human! All the squeezes for my "seasonal" friend!

CHAPTER 1

RAFE

"It's everywhere, Ian. No matter where I turn, it's pumpkin spiced everything! I seriously cannot escape it." Turning to check for cars before crossing the street, I talked on the phone via the Bluetooth device that rarely left my right ear. "I don't care how tasty it is, why can't we at least make it through September before we're knee deep in pumpkins? That's all I want to know."

I eased my way through the crowd of people on the sidewalk. I ignored the stares and odd glances passed my way from the idiots who didn't see the blinking light of the earpiece I wore. I walked around the corner, ducking my head as I passed under the low red awning over the front door of Fairytale Florals. I grinned I as saw Ian sitting next door at a table he'd saved for us at The Glazed Bun.

Glancing across the tables that formed the patio seating

area, his eyes flicked over the other patrons until he saw me. I waved a hand silently with an amused smirk. Ian turned off his own phone, dropping it down on the table in front of him as I made my way over to join him.

"What? You can't even say good-bye before you hang up the phone? Ass." I laughed as I slipped into the empty seat across from Ian.

"Kinda pointless to say good-bye when I'll be saying hello a few seconds later, don't you think?" Ian smirked. "Hello, Rafe."

"Oh, shut it. Did you order coffee yet?" I looked around for the server, anxious to get a dose of caffeine.

"Yep. I ordered you a pumpkin spice latte." Ian threw his blonde head back and laughed at the stony glare on my face. "Chill out, Rafe. They're bringing coffee out soon. I'm just screwing with you."

The waiter came up right then, a tiny little red-headed omega with bright green eyes and an even brighter smile. Efficiently setting empty coffee mugs in front of us, he then put a slim silver carafe of coffee in the center of the table.

Digging into the front, waist level pouch of his shamrock green apron, he chirped at us in a nasal sing-song voice: "Hey, cuties! Meet Tom! Tom is all yours today." With a sly wink he added as he openly checked us both out, "Your server, that is. Tom's number is negotiable, but let's get through breakfast first, m'kay?"

I grinned up at the sassy little guy as he pulled packets of sugar and containers of creamer out of the apron pocket. With a quirked brow, I leered at him suggestively. "Well, I really hope that number is negotiable if you're already giving up your cream."

Tom looked at me with his head tilted slightly, as if sizing me up. With a nod, he said: "You'll do. And baby, Tom would never give up the cream at the first meet-cute. And definitely not until after someone buys Tom a drink or three! Let Tom just put that right out there, m'kay?"

He pulled out the menus that had been clamped under his arm and set one in front of each of us. Ian caught the omega's small, delicate hand as he put the menu down on the table. Stroking his thumb over the back of Tom's hand, Ian asked with a flirtatious wink: "Can I hear more about this giving up of your cream? And how soon can I buy Tom a drink or three?"

Tom winked and pulled his hand back. Pointing at me and then back to Ian, he said: "Oh, you two are trouble! Good thing Tom loves trouble, right? Now be a couple of good little alphas for Tom and look over your menus. Tom will be back soon to take your orders, m'kay?" He blew a noisy kiss at us and sauntered away, swinging his round little butt as he went. The black uniform trousers hugged his curvy globes to perfection, and Tom obviously knew how to work that to his advantage.

Ian drew in a sharp breath and said: "Dibs."

I shook my head with a grin. Casually, I reached for the carafe and began to pour myself a cup of coffee as I spoke. "Dibs? Seriously, Ian? You do realize that Tom is a person and not the last piece of pie at Thanksgiving, right?"

"Yeah, and I also realize that I got here first and waited forever for your slow ass to show up. For making me wait, I get dibs. Plus, let's be honest. That little twink would eat you for dinner." Ian's matter-of-fact words combined with the earnest expression on his face totally cracked me up.

My eyes narrowed as I shook my head. "Fair point. Now hurry up and pick out what you want to eat. I have an appointment with the realtor after this." I added a cream and two packets of sugar to my coffee before finally taking a drink. "Ah. Nectar of the gods. I tell you, I don't know how non-coffee drinkers survive the day."

Ian watched me affectionately, his fingertips tapping out a steady rhythm on the tabletop. "Realtor, huh? I guess that means that you're putting down roots and sticking around here in Hollydale?"

I nodded with a shrug. "I've been thinking about it, and you're right. There's nothing left for me back home, and I can write anywhere. But I need to get my own place. No offense, Ian, but your couch just isn't that comfortable."

"Yeah, but the rent on it is more than fair." His green eyes glinted with pleasure at the idea of my moving here permanently. He'd been bugging me to make this move for the past several months now.

"Zero price for zero comfort? That's more than fair, I suppose." I tilted my head and looked up at the clear blue sky overhead as I pretended to think for a minute. I looked back over at Ian and said with a shrug: "No. In fact, you should be paying me for sleeping on it. The massage bills and chiropractor fees alone are more than what a month's rent at a decent hotel would be.

"Yeah, I suppose it would seem that way." Ian nodded in fake agreement. "Except that I'm not paying for your happy endings. You can pay your own masseuse bills, my friend. And the decent hotel wouldn't have my charming face and a fridge full of beer."

"Ah, good point. Forgot about the beer. Well, anyway, I'm meeting up with a realtor to see what is up for sale around this tiny town. I don't have the highest of hopes that anything here will compare to my place back home though. I don't mean to sound like an ass, it's just that there are more amenities in the city."

Ian shot me a wry grin. "True that. However, what we lack in amenities, we make up for with loads of charm." He waved his hand as if showcasing the row of cute little shops that lined the small main street around us.

Tom came bustling over to take our order. He must

have been in a rush, because there was a minimum of sass before he zipped off again after making sure that we were good on coffee.

As Tom was heading our way with an expertly balanced tray a little while later, Ian was saying: "You know what you need, Rafe? You need a night out. Let's go to the bar tonight, have some drinks, and let you experience the local nightlife before you become a resident of our fair town."

"Does this place even have a gay friendly bar or club? Because I'm not exactly in the mood to deal with a bunch of ignorant rednecks or turn down lonely ladies all night. No offense."

Tom set our food down as I was speaking. After he'd emptied the tray, he hugged it to his chest as he bounced up and down on the balls of his feet.

"Oh! Tom knows the perfect place!" He turned to Ian, his lithe frame practically vibrating with excitement. "Have you been to the O-zone Lair?" At Ian's smiling nod, Tom turned back to me and explained.

"The O-zone Lair is an Alpha/Omega friendly club. The downstairs is low-key, but upstairs? Oh, my lands! Honey, you and those killer green eyes would be in serious trouble upstairs."

He looked around then leaned in closer to speak in a stage whisper. "Tom loves the freaky party upstairs!"

Standing tall again, he turned to Ian. Fluttering his eyelashes, he pouted a bit before talking in a fast clip.

"Are you two studs going there tonight? Tom is always up for a night at the big O. Tom has the cutest little omega friend that really needs to put down his book and get out for a night on the town too. That is, if you would like some help convincing your buddy here that Hollydale isn't a completely boring little burg?"

Ian flicked a glance in my direction. At my slight nod, he held out his phone to Tom. "Put your digits in, baby boy. I'll text you when we know what time we're heading over, if that's okay?"

Tom took his phone and tapped the screen with a flurry of his fingers. "Here you go, lover boy. Tom just hopes that this wasn't a misguided attempt to get Tom's number and then leave Tom sad and lonely on a Saturday night when you're too shy to show up."

Ian's mouth dropped open. "Have people actually done that to Tom?" I grinned as Ian automatically fell in with Tom's habit of speaking of himself in the third person. Ian took his phone, catching Tom's fingers in his as he did.

"I would never do that to a beauty like Tom. Now tell me baby, can Tom really bring a friend for my buddy Rafe over there tonight? Because I think I'm gonna be busy letting Tom show Ian here the second floor." Ian pulled Tom's fingers up to his mouth and kissed those delicate fingertips before releasing them.

Tom giggled as Ian's eyes still roamed brazenly over that trim little body. "Ooh, Ian." He was downright purring at this point. "Tom is just going to have so much fun showing Ian the second floor!" He turned to me then. Tilting his head thoughtfully, Tom looked me over one more time. "Okay, Tom will make Milo come out tonight and meet Rafe. This will be fun, Tom promises that Rafe will enjoy the big O."

After Tom left us to eat our food, I rolled my eyes at Ian. "The O-zone Lair? Seriously? And do I want to know what goes on up on the second floor?"

Ian winked at me. "There's a reason why the locals call it the big O, and it's not an abbreviation. That's all I'm saying, if you catch my drift. But hey, just stay downstairs and have some boring vanilla fun with Tom's buddy. There's a full bar, a dance floor, and from what it sounds like, the company of a pleasant little bookworm omega. Which is the perfect date for a writer. What could possibly go wrong?"

I took a bite of my spinach omelet and rolled my eyes. I couldn't begin to list the things that could go wrong, but I knew that Ian would have a rebuttal for every argument that I could name. No, it was just easier to go along with it. Ian and I both knew that he'd win in the end anyway. Besides, who knows? Maybe I'd actually have fun tonight.

CHAPTER 2

MILO

"I'm not going out with a random alpha that you don't even know, Tom. Are you kidding me?" I took off my glasses and used my shirt to wipe the smudge currently clouding the right lens. Tom was stretched backwards over my couch, his legs draped artfully up over the back while his head hung off the edge of the cushions. I guess Tom liked looking at the world upside down. Or head rushes. Either way, it didn't look at all comfortable to me.

"Ugh. Tom promised the alphas that he would bring Milo! Milo owes Tom for helping to roll a billion and one fudge balls last weekend! Milo promised that Tom could name whatever favor Tom wanted in return. Tom is calling in the favor. Besides. Rafe is totally hot! Tom would never try to hook Milo up with an uggo alpha."

Tom shivered at the thought of setting me up with an unattractive alpha. Of course, that's only because if he did, then he would have to look at him when we all went out. Or, goddess forbid, what if people possibly thought that he was the one with the fugly alpha on his arm?

I sat up tall in my chair, picking idly at a loose thread on the side of my jeans. "I don't have an actual choice in this, do I? You're totally dragging me out on this date, even if you have to roofie me to do it. Am I right? I mean, I should just go along with it already because we both know that you're going to win in the end anyway."

With smooth fluidity that I would never possess, Tom lifted his legs and flipped over to a sitting position. "Tom is relieved that Milo finally has seen the light. Now let's go see what can be pulled together into an acceptable outfit out of that frightening closet in there. Tom does not have high hopes! Still, Tom will try."

I rolled my eyes as Tom stood and walked across the small room to my bedroom. He turned on the light and went over to help himself to my closet. From my vantage point, I could easily watch as he stood there flipping through my closet and muttering to himself. When clothes began flying over his shoulder willy-nilly and piling up wherever they happened to land, I decided that enough was enough.

With a light sigh, I stood and wearily walked to my room. "Tom, do we really need to throw everything out onto the floor and bed? Honestly, man. I had all my clothes sorted by color and separated according to season. Now I just have a mess to pick up!"

Tom turned his head, eyeing me disdainfully as he waved a negligent hand in the direction of my discarded wardrobe. "Tom does not consider those rags to be worthy of being called clothes. Forget reorganizing them, just bag them up and toss them in the incinerator. Do not dare try to donate them either! The poor have enough to worry about without being dressed like myopic gypsy trolls on top of it."

I huffed out an indignant puff of air. "Words fail me, Tom. I cannot believe you sometimes. Seriously. And just where exactly am I supposed to afford this grand new wardrobe that you think I need?"

Tom looked back over at me. He actually seemed a bit guilty. I watched as his pale cheeks flushed red to match his hair. "Tom did not think about Milo's money problems. Tom is sorry. But good news! Tom found a not completely objectionable outfit for Milo to wear."

He handed me a pair of black skinny jeans that I hadn't worn since the day I'd bought them in 2013. I'd worn them just long enough to decide that fashion wasn't worth having my nuts pinched in a denim vise all day. After the jeans, he tossed over a soft, dark purple t-shirt with a deep V-neck.

"Tom! That shirt is from high school! Seriously, that's

like a relic of my thankfully short-lived goth days. I can't wear that."

"Milo will look yummy in this shirt. Get those pants off. Tom needs to see if they will fit that bubble butt of Milo's."

I rolled my eyes but just went along with Tom's orders. It really was faster since I'd end up giving in later anyway. "And for the record," I said as I pulled the painfully tight pants up over my thighs. "There were only 350 fudge balls that needed rolling. And I offered to pay you, so don't think that you're going to get away with blackmailing with it again after tonight."

After I got the pants over my cheeks, I carefully tucked in my junk before pulling up the zipper. They were a snug fit, but not nearly as tight as I'd remembered. Huh. Guess all the long hours standing in the kitchen have helped me out. Either that, or it was from the low appetite I'd had lately. First there was the grief of my father dying and then the stress of finding out that his lavish lifestyle had been heavily mortgaged.

No. Tonight I wasn't going to stress about losing the family home or how I was going to keep Sweet Ballz in business if Auntie G's Candy Shoppe didn't back down soon. Nope. Tonight, I was going to go out with Tom and these two alphas he'd dug up for us, and I was going to have fun for a change. I was about to ask Tom their names again when his phone rang.

While Tom answered the phone, he pointed at a pair of slim, black ankle boots with a cute side zipper. I nodded and grabbed them along with a pair of black socks. I finished getting dressed and went to style my hair while Tom finished his call. From the heavy flirting, I guessed it was the alpha that he had made the date with tonight.

With a soft sigh, I got myself mentally prepared for this date. I just had to be nice long enough to drink a beer. Once Tom disappeared with his date, I could make my excuses and duck home to finish the new Rake McFeely novel that I'd downloaded this morning. I knew from experience that Tom would definitely take off. Unless this alpha was more interesting than the book, I would plan to be home early enough for a full night of reading.

CHAPTER 3
RAFE

"I'm not gonna stay here alone all night with some random little omega while you get your freak on upstairs, Ian. Just letting you know that straight up." I took of pull of my beer, watching the door for Tom to make his entrance with my blind date that he'd scrounged up for me.

A blind date. For me. An alpha with a hefty trust fund and a full head of hair in the prime of my life? Yeah. Like I really needed to be set up? I grinned and shook my head. Somehow, I'd been steamrolled into this evening, but at least I was out of Ian's apartment and among other people for a change.

I happened to glance across the bar right as the tiny ginger dynamo flounced in the door. With a grin, I nudged Ian and tilted my head in Tom's direction. "Don't look now, but your date's here."

Ian slid off his bar stool and headed off without a word to me. I sat there and finished my beer while I watched Ian and Tom greeting each other with a little more familiarity than their brief acquaintance would have indicated. I shook my head, about ready to just call it a night and sneak out the back when I looked behind Tom.

Holy shit. The most adorable little nerd that I'd ever seen was standing there shyly behind Tom. His jeans were painted on, and the V-neck of his shirt was teasing me with a hint of his milky flesh. I'd always been a sucker for guys with glasses too. He was a guy definitely worth meeting. I just hoped that the person inside matched the cuteness on the outside. In my experience, the two usually didn't match up at all.

I slid off my stool and left the empty on the bar with enough cash to cover our beers and a tip. As I was walking over, Ian looked around for me. When he realized that I was headed their direction, he took Tom's arm and looked around the room as if trying to locate a table. Tom pointed to an empty table on the far side of the dance floor, and we all changed course to head over there.

They beat me to the table but were just taking their seats when I got there. Tom had maneuvered himself and Ian on one side of the table. His omega friend scooted over to the farthest seat across from them, leaving the front one open for me.

Ignoring the other two idiots who were already eye-fucking each other, I sat down and held out a hand in greeting. "Hi, I'm Rafe. I see you've already met my friend, Ian."

"Milo," he said, taking my hand and shaking it with a sure grip. "I'm Tom's friend. It's nice to meet you, Rafe."

I reluctantly let his hand go, already entranced by the guy. He nervously licked his full, pink lips. "Would you like a drink?" I asked him, thinking a little social lubricant might be in order.

"Ooh!" Tom squealed before Milo could answer. "Tom definitely needs a drinkie! Good idea, alpha-boy! Drinkies for everyone!" He waved widely in our direction before he turned back to Ian. "Let's go, lover boy! Tom will go fetch first round, m'kay? Milo and Rafe can wait here and hold the table. Ian and Tom will be back soon!"

I watched them go, then turned to Milo and asked: "What are the chances that they actually remember to bring back our drinks?"

Milo snorted and rolled his eyes. "The odds are not in our favor, I'm afraid."

I nodded and waved the waitress over. "I guess we'll just have to look out for ourselves then."

A couple of beers later, our friends still hadn't made

their appearance. Milo carefully took the last bite of the nachos that we had been sharing in the meantime. I loved how his eyes would close every time he took a bite. It was as if Milo were blocking the world out as he savored the flavor of what he was eating.

With a gulp, I pushed away the thought of what face he might make if something a little bigger were in his mouth. "So, Milo. Please don't take this the wrong way, but do you wanna get out of here? I'm pretty sure that we've been ditched and this whole bar thing really isn't my scene.

Milo looked around the crowded bar, blushing as his eyes passed over the seven huge silver birdcages that were placed strategically around the room. Each cage held a glitter painted omega dressed only in a matching glittery jock. The caged omegas danced and gyrated for tips while alphas crowded around them. I'm not gonna say that they weren't hot as hell to look at, but I'd been telling the truth when I'd said that this wasn't my scene.

Turning his attention back to me, Milo nodded hesitantly. I stood and tossed some cash down on the table for our server. Milo stood and shyly took the hand that I held out in a silent offer. My large hand wrapped around his smaller hand. He wasn't that much shorter than me, maybe a few inches tops, but our body types were completely different.

Milo had fine bones and a slender physique where I was solid and thick. I wasn't as burly or tall as many other alphas, but next to Milo I definitely felt like an alpha. He was just so sweet, and innocently pure. At least, that was the vibe he gave. I held the door for him as we walked out into the night.

"Did you drive here? Because I rode with Ian." I said after we got outside away from the noise.

"Actually, Tom and I ubered here in case we drank too much." The street lights reflected off of his glasses, blocking my view of his pretty brown eyes.

"Well, it's a nice night and I don't have anywhere to be. Do you feel like just walking around and talking?" I figured he would feel much safer if he knew that I genuinely wanted to get to know him, not just get down his tight pants.

"Honestly? That sounds perfect, and way more me than anything in there." He nodded back toward the O-zone with a shy smile.

I nodded in agreement. "Exactly. This is more me too. Hey, I work from home, I'm not exactly used to crowds. Heck, sometimes just being around Ian is too much peopling for me in a day."

His lilting giggle was charming. I smiled over at him as he asked: "Wow, I didn't know that you work from home. People really do that, huh? Well, I'm not around people much either. I spend my days in the kitchen."

"Yeah, people really do that." I replied. "Kitchen

worker, huh? Do you work at the restaurant where we met Tom this morning?"

Milo shook his head. "No, I own a local candy store. We make all of the candy there on the premises. It keeps me pretty much chained in the kitchen some days. But yeah, I'm the one in the back covered in sugar."

"Seriously? That's really cool, Milo! Is your shop here in Hollydale? I'd love to see it sometime. What's the name?"

"Yep, it's right here in town. It's actually just a few shops down from The Glazed Bun where Tom works. It's called Sweet Ballz. And yes, you should definitely come check it out the next time you're down that way."

"I'm definitely going to take you up on that invitation. You have no idea the size of my sweet tooth." I smiled over at him, gently squeezing his hand that I still held.

"So, what do you do then, Rafe? You mentioned that you work from home?"

"Yeah. Well, I can actually work wherever I am, as long as I have my laptop along. I'm a writer. I've been doing it for a few years now." I shrugged, not trying to impress him by going into any more detail than that.

"Really? Do you use your own name or a pen? What kind of books do you write? Oh, man, sorry if I'm rambling. I'm just an obsessive reader, like you have no idea! I read pretty much everything. I'm just dying to know if you've written anything that I may have read."

"Well, if you're an omegaverse romance fan, then you probably have read at least one of my books."

Milo stopped in his tracks. "Are you saying that to trick me or are you serious? I mean, did Tom put you up to saying that? Because I'm a huge reader of that trope! I've probably read just about everything out there that's worth reading."

"Okay. Well, nobody put me up to telling you this, I promise! It's actually a bit of a surprise that I am, because it's something that very few people know about me. But here goes. I'm gonna throw out a few titles and you tell me if you know who I am." I winked at him and at his excited nod, began to list some of my top-rated titles. "The Alpha's Last Stand", "The Virgin Omega", "An Alpha to Remember", "Fated to Him"? Do any of those ring a bell for you?"

Milo was practically vibrating at this point. "No! You are not Rake McFeely! No, you can't be! No!"

I grinned, happy that he'd recognized my book titles. "So, which of those have you read? Do you have a favorite?"

"What? Are you seriously kidding me with that? Rafe! I've read all of them! No kidding! If you're ever over at my apartment, I'll show you my e-reader. I own all of your books, I think. In fact, I was planning to ditch out early tonight, so I could get home and read your new book! I just downloaded it this morning. Wait. Is that weird? I hope this doesn't freak you out that I'm totally fanboying out on you right now." He bit into his bottom lip anxiously as he waited for my response.

"Why would it be weird? It's not like you knew who I was when you came out tonight, right? But, umm, if you could keep it on the down-low, I'd appreciate it. I use an anonymous pen name for a reason. My family would flip out if they knew what I really did with my days." I wasn't joking either.

"Why is that? And what exactly is it that your family thinks that you do?" He looked at me with curious eyes.

"My family thinks that I'm a lazy playboy frittering my life away from party to party while maintaining my proper place in society. Because as a member of the Smythe family, that is all that is required. Well, that and take time at some point to father an heir and a spare. But to actually do something common such as earn money? And with my own ingenuity? Perish the thought, dahling." I laughed then, fully aware of how brittle it sounded.

"Oh, Rafe. That's disgusting. I'm so sorry that your family doesn't appreciate you. Do you see your family very often?" Milo's look of concern was melting me.

"No. There's not many of us left, to be honest. My dad passed away last year, and my mother is flitting around

Europe with my kid brother these days. I'm not really a fan of the extended relations, so I stay out of their sphere as much as possible. Ian is more family to me than my actual family is, to tell the truth. What about your family?"

Milo nodded pensively, his lips pursed. "My alpha dad, he died last year too. I'm kinda still digging out from under the mess that he left behind. My omega dad died when I was young. It's funny, my family was one of the founding families of Hollydale, but I'm the only one left now. Tom is my Ian, if you know what I mean."

I stopped walking and pulled Milo in for a hug. "Then I guess you and I are pretty much in the same boat, except that somewhere out there I have an absentee mother and a younger brother flitting about in her wake."

Milo pulled wrapped his arms around my neck and hugged me back. The wind shifted and for the first time, I was able to catch his personal omega scent. I almost laughed out loud when I realized that the cute little omega who had captured my attention smelled like pumpkin spice. I couldn't wait to tell Ian, he was gonna die.

"Hey, Rafe? Please don't take this the wrong way. It's just that I'm cold. But I'm really not done talking to you yet. So, I was wondering," he paused and took a fortifying breath before continuing his thought. "Would you like to go back to my place?"

CHAPTER 4
MILO

"I'm serious, Tom! Nothing happened! He came home with me, I made us coffee and we hung out." I crossed my fingers since Tom couldn't see that through the phone.

"Honestly, Milo. Tom sets you up with a good looking, available alpha and Milo just takes the alpha home for coffee? Did Milo at least serve cream with the coffee? That special omega cream?"

"Stop it, Tom! Don't be gross. We just talked and got to know each other better. He's taking me to dinner tonight, if that makes you feel better."

"Tom approves. Does Milo know what to wear for this date tonight?"

I sighed. That right there was why I hadn't wanted to tell Tom about my date this evening. It had taken me half the morning to put all the clothes away that he'd tried to trash the day before. "Don't worry, Tom. I've got it under control. Besides, it's just dinner because I have to work tomorrow."

Tom huffed in my ear. "All Milo does is work. Now, let Tom tell Milo about what happened last night with Ian. Milo will approve!"

"Actually, Tom? I doubt that I'll approve. You took off and left me there with a stranger! He turned out to be nice, but what if he hadn't? And it's not like you even know Ian either! You literally just met them yesterday! What were you thinking, Tom?"

"Milo, darling. It is not *what* Tom was thinking, but rather what Tom was thinking *with*, to be quite blunt. And let Tom assure Milo that the little head is usually the better head to listen to in these situations."

I groaned and tuned out the rest of Tom's conversation. I really didn't want to hear the blow-by-blow, pun *not* intended, of his evening with Ian. After a few more minutes, I rushed him off the phone and hurried to take a shower. I really did want to look my best tonight. I wasn't ready to admit it to Tom, but Rafe was the best alpha I'd ever met. He was smart, sweet, and gorgeous. Which probably meant that he was too good to be true, but whatever. I was willing to take a risk if it meant spending another evening with him.

"Okay, one more and that's it. Seriously. Not another bite." I bit into the garlicky goodness and closed my eyes to enjoy the food-gasm it gave me. So yummy!

Rafe laughed at me as I ate another garlic fry after saying the same thing that I'd been saying for the last ten or so bites. I really was full, it's just that the food was so fricken yummy.

This time though, I wiped my fingertips on the napkin, laid it over the plate and pushed it away. I had to stop, or I would be sick. "What did you want to do next?"

Rafe wiggled his eyebrows and smirked at me. "Are you sure you want to ask a loaded question like that, cutie?"

I blushed furiously as I adjusted my glasses. "Okay, I admit it. That was a loaded question. I meant, would you like to walk around like we did last time? Or maybe check out the bowling alley, or something along those lines. I would offer to go back to my place and watch a movie, but after that last comment I'm thinking maybe I'll just leave that off the table."

Rafe's teeth gleamed as he grinned. "Actually, a walk does sound good after all that food we just consumed. But if you want to go back to your place and watch a movie after that, I promise to be a good little alpha."

Shaking my head, I said: "Why does that sound like famous last words?" After a brief argument, I paid the bill and we left the diner. It was windier tonight. I walked with my arms hugging my waist, as I fought off the chill. Without warning, Rafe's jacket landed around my shoulders.

"Put it on, Milo. I'm not gonna be responsible for you freezing to death out here. I don't think that would be a romantic end to our date, do you?" He winked at me and waited to see me put it on.

I shrugged my arms into the over-sized jacket and zipped it up. Without thinking, I blurted out: "Oh, so this is definitely a date then? I wasn't sure."

"Well, then allow me to clarify it for you." Rafe stepped in front of me and put his hands on either side of my face then leaned in and kissed me gently. Pulling away, he winked and asked: "Did that clear things up for you, Milo?"

"Hmm. I dunno, Rafe. I may need to go over that again later if the details get fuzzy." I shocked myself by easily flirting with the hot alpha, but with him I wasn't nervous for some reason.

We walked through town at an easy pace. When we got near my neighborhood, I reached out for his hand. "Why don't we go back to my place now, and watch a movie or something? It's pretty chilly out here anyway."

At his easy agreement, we headed toward my place. Before I knew it, we were in my living room and snuggled up on my couch. I let Rafe control the remote while we searched for a movie. I didn't really care what he chose, I was just enjoying being with him. There was just something about him that drew me in and made me want to get closer to him.

After we agreed on a classic comedy, Rafe set the remote on the coffee table and stretched his arm out for me to snuggle up to him. After a brief moment of hesitation, I scooted over and cuddled up against him. His arm went around my back, with his hand coming to rest on my hip. It was way more couple-ish than I would have expected for a second date, but I definitely wasn't complaining.

By the time the movie ended, neither of us were watching it. At some point, I'd ended up on Rafe's lap for a kiss and then we'd been busy playing tonsil hockey for the second half of the movie. When the room went silent, I managed to pull my lips apart from his long enough to look over my shoulder at the TV. The movie had ended, and we were back at the information screen that detailed the flick.

I laughed and touched my forehead down against Rafe's shoulder. "Did we just miss the entire movie to make out, or did I imagine that?"

His lips kissed the top of my head as he chuckled into my hair. "Yeah, we pretty much did exactly that. But it was fun, right?"

Suddenly things got a little too serious for me. I felt the sexual tension in the room, and I wasn't ready to make that step yet. I hadn't told him yet that I'm still a virgin, but he's probably figured it out. I wanted it, I really did. I just wasn't ready. Even with an alpha like Rafe.

I sat up and looked around for my glasses. As if reading my mind, Rafe plucked them up from the end table next to him and glided them onto my face slowly. "I think it's time for me to go, Milo. Either that, or I won't be willing to leave. And although I'd love it, I somehow doubt that you're ready for that yet, Milo."

I shook my head slowly, looking down at my lap. "I'm sorry, Rafe."

Rafe put two fingers under my chin and tilted my face up to look into my eyes. "Milo. Never be sorry for being true to yourself. You're right. It is too soon, and we don't need to rush. When you're ready, I'll be here. If you're never ready, I'll still be here, enjoying your company. I'm not gonna lie, Milo. I mean, you're sexy as fuck, baby. But that doesn't mean that I would ever push you into something that you're not ready to do."

I blushed at his words, then slowly nodded. "Thanks, Rafe. I'm not used to alphas that aren't pushy or trying to force their will on me."

Rafe smiled and kissed my forehead. "I'm not most alphas, Milo. I'd rather that we take our time and really build something. I don't know why, but I have a really good feeling about you."

CHAPTER 5

RAFE

TWO WEEKS LATER

"I've got to find something soon, Ian. This is getting stupid. Everything I've looked at is too small, too funky, too overpriced for what's there, or just too whatever."

I sighed as I walked around the corner and headed for Sweet Ballz to meet Milo. "I'm about to walk into Milo's shop now. I'll catch up with you later, okay?"

I clicked the off button on my earpiece and walked into Milo's candy store. Every time I walked in, I was taken back to another era. The walls were painted with vertical pastel pink and mint green stripes. The color theme continued with mint green floor tiles and pink vinyl covered cushions on the white metal chairs that were spaced around the handful of small white tables.

The counter area was all glass and chrome, with large display cases to show off all the wonderful varieties of candy that Milo had available. The kid that Milo had working the counter for the afternoon was dressed like a 1950's soda jerk. The pristine all-white outfit of a short-sleeved button up shirt and pants were topped off by a long, rectangular paper hat that sat jauntily on his head. The shop was adorable, just like it's owner.

I stepped up to the counter, squinting to read the kid's name tag. I knew Milo wasn't far away. His pumpkin spice scent was overpoweringly strong. I don't know how it took me so long to smell it in the first place, it's that strong. "Hey, there. Umm," I said squinting to read the name tag, squinting and squinting...oh! There it was! "Kent. Hello. I'm looking for Milo."

The kid looked at me curiously as he scratched at a pimple on his jaw. "Umm. He's, like, in back? But I'm pretty sure that you can't go back there." He looked at me with vacant eyes as he prodded more at the zit.

"Yeah, Kent. I get that. Would you please just go tell him that Rafe is here is to see him?" I resisted the urge to roll my eyes.

"But I'm like, uh, not supposed to leave the counter." I looked into his dull eyes and said: "Kent, I am the only person here right now. Take ten seconds and go ask Milo to come out or if I can go back. Please? I will watch out for any customers while you are gone, I promise."

He looked at me as if unsure what to do. I nodded my

head with what I hoped resembled an encouraging smile as I pointed toward the door to the kitchen. "Go ahead, Kent. I'll wait right here."

He walked to the door and disappeared. I figured it was fifty-fifty as to whether he remembered what I'd sent him back there to do. A few minutes later, Kent came back through the swinging door. "Umm. Milo's in the kitchen, but I dunno if he wants to see anyone right now."

"Did you tell him that I was here?" I was getting irritated with this useless idiot. I'd been seeing Milo every day for the past couple weeks, it's not as if the dumbass hadn't seen me in here before.

"Umm. No? Because he's like crying and stuff? I didn't know what to do." His hand went back to the zit as he stood there staring at me.

I went around the counter at that point, edging around the not so helpful employee. "I'm going back there, Kent. Don't worry, if he gets pissed I'll be sure to let him know that you tried to stop me."

Before I went through the door I looked back at the kid and said firmly: "And Kent? Go wash your nasty hands. You don't ever touch your face, especially to pick a damn zit, when you're working with food. Think about it. It's just gross, dude."

I left Kent to hopefully wash his hands in the sink behind the counter where they washed their scoops and utensils. After I passed through the door, I stepped into a surprisingly modern kitchen area. As advertised, Milo was sitting at a long metal counter with his face in his hands and crying his heart out.

I went right over and pulled up the stool beside him. I set my messenger bag down on the table and sat down. Reaching out, I put my arms around his shoulders and pulled him up against me. His glasses lay on the table in front of him, on top of a letter. I didn't try to read the letter, but I couldn't miss the law firm letterhead at the top. I'd know that letterhead anywhere, it was from the law office whose managing partner was Ian's father.

Rubbing small circles on his back, I petted and comforted Milo until his crying slowed. "Are you okay, Milo? Do you want to talk about it?" I asked softly, not wanting to overstep or make him cry again.

"N-n-no. It's just an issue with a c-c-competitor. B-but I'd rather not talk about it right now. I'll figure it out. I just got overwhelmed for a bit there." His stuttering breaths began to calm. His head rested on my shoulder and I felt his hot breath against my neck.

"Okay. Well, how about I take you to lunch then? Or can you leave? No offense, but I'm not sure if I would leave Kent in charge of the place while you left anyway."

Milo laughed and sat back onto his own stool, his tear-streaked face lighting up. "I know. That kid is helpless.

I keep hoping he'll get better, but I don't see him improving. I just feel bad firing him. He means well, you know? Besides, the next kid I'd find to hire would be just as bad. The pickings are not so great in this little town."

"So, I had planned to sit in your pretty little candy parlor and do some writing until you close up for the day. Would you rather that I hang out back here instead? I can keep you company while you work if you want." It surprised me that I was nervously waiting for an answer. In the short amount of time that we'd known each other, Milo had become all too important to me.

"Hmm. Do you take instruction well, Rafe? Can you handle getting bossed around by an omega?" Milo looked at me with assessing eyes. "I actually have a large order of PBF Bombz that I need to fill today, if you'd like to help me."

I jumped up from my stool. "Really? I can help? That's so cool! Of course, I can take direction from you, Milo. What, do I look like an alpha-douche or something? Wait. What's PBF?"

Milo giggled and stood, taking a step closer to me. "Let's go with *or something*. And PBF is Peanut Butter Fudge. Don't worry, I'll give you some extra to take home. I'm not completely cruel."

I narrowed my eyes and grabbed his hips. When I lifted

him, his hands went right to my shoulders and hung on. I spun in a circle, laughing up into his face that hovered over mine. Our eyes caught, and the laughs subsided as the air grew thicker between us.

Milo slid down my body as I lowered him to the floor. We stood there breathless. We were pressed together, chest to chest and face to face. His hands remained on my shoulders, mine on his hips. Our lips finally clashed together after a few days, or several seconds, who could really tell at that point.

My thought processes came to a full stop. I couldn't think at all. I could only feel. I felt the soft velvet of Milo's tongue dancing with mine. I felt the fluttering on my cheek from his eyelashes. I felt each exhaled burst of warm breath from his nostrils. I felt his heart pounding against my chest, where mine was pounding too. I felt the grip of Milo's hands on my shoulders as he clung to me. But more than anything, I felt the bar of steel that was pressed against my hip.

I broke the kiss as soon as I regained my senses. Panting, I looked into his eyes that were blown wide with lust. "Milo. Babe. We have to stop. I'm pretty sure this isn't food grade behavior, yeah?"

Milo snorted out a laugh as he took a step back. "Yeah, the county inspector probably wouldn't approve." He looked thoughtfully at the ceiling for a moment then back at me with a laugh. "Actually though? He probably would. He's a creepy alpha that would probably give me a full A+ rating if I let him sit and watch."

When he saw my bugged-out eyes and open mouth, Milo laughed harder. The little shit pulled his phone out of his pocket and snapped a pic. I grabbed for his phone, but he shrugged away with a giggle and commented: "Hey, I just took a picture, so it would last longer! Isn't that the usual advice?"

"Milo? If that winds up on social media..."

Before I could finish the threat, Milo chortled and skirted around me. "Social media? Screw that! This is going on my holiday cards this year!"

A short time later I found myself washed, gloved, hair netted and wrapped in a huge pink apron. Milo had given me a warning glare as he put the apron on me and tied the strings, so I hadn't said a word. Anything I'd said would have been in fun anyway. I didn't care what I was wearing. I was just enjoying being here with Milo in this moment and sharing his work with him.

Milo cleaned the work station, then brought over a huge bowl of something gooey and peanut buttery from the industrial refrigerator at the back of the room. After a quick demonstration of how to properly form a ball and roll it smoothly into the uniform size that Milo required, he left me to it. While I made the balls, Milo melted chocolate in a double boiler at the big stove that stood a few feet away from the work surface where I was stationed.

I saw him whisking in a pinch of this and a dash of that but had no idea what he'd used. It was definitely a new side of Milo, to see him confidently moving around the kitchen. Once the chocolate was prepared, he brought it over and set it across from me. He laid out trays lined with wax paper. Milo sat down then and picked up a pair of tongs. I watched as he dipped the balls I'd rolled into the chocolate mixture.

With deft flicks of his wrist, he dipped and placed each ball on the prepared trays. He caught up with me quickly. Once I finished my job, I started cleaning my mess while he finished his part of the job. As I worked, I thought about how amazing it was that every time I learned something new about Milo, it only made me more interested in him.

CHAPTER 6

MILO

"I'm serious, Tom. I don't want Rafe to know about my problems with Auntie G's. What if he thinks she's telling the truth and that I really did steal my PBF Bombz recipe from her?" I chewed my lip and looked down at the cafe table where I sat with Tom.

"Milo. Rafe would never believe that Milo would steal a recipe from that lying skank. As if." Tom curled his lip in disgust. He was always my champion defender, but this mess with Auntie G's had him particularly riled. "Anybody who knows Milo knows better than to believe this pack of lies. And if Rafe did believe it? Then screw Rafe because Rafe would not be the alpha that Tom thinks Rafe is."

I looked up at Tom, my eyes blinking rapidly as I fought to follow his sentence. Sometimes Tom's lack of pronoun usage got really awkward. Running my hands over my face, I shuddered out a sigh. "I know. I just, well, I don't want him to think that he has to rush in and save the day or something. All I need to do is find my Nana's recipe book and show it to my attorney. We have sixty days to fight the cease and desist order, or I'll lose the rights to the recipe forever. He said that the age alone of the family recipe would do a lot to prove my claim, along with your statement of helping me make these for as long as you can remember. Which, by the way, I appreciate."

Tom rolled his eyes and waved a hand at me in a shooing gesture. "Omega, please. Nana made those PBF balls when Milo and Tom were in diapers. Tom's lucky that there are no pudgy pictures from a childhood spent eating those little fat pills. The only change that Milo made is to the name. And Tom stated that in the deposition."

I nodded and took a drink of my latte. "Well, still. Thank you, Tom. You're a good friend and you've always had my back. But I have to save this recipe. Not only is it my top seller, but it's special to me because it was Nana's."

Tom nodded mournfully. "So, what is Milo going to do? Milo doesn't have the recipe book, and thanks to Milo's dad, Milo no longer owns the family home. This is a problem." Tom's worried expression touched me. I reached over and grabbed his hand.

"I have a plan." Tom looked at me skeptically but waited for me to explain. "The house won't finish escrow until next week. Tomorrow night, I'm going to sneak in and go look through Nana's stuff in the attic. That's the only place it could be."

Tom shook his head and began to interrupt, but I held a hand up and continued: "Dad packed up her personal things when she passed away and put them up in the attic by her mother's oak wardrobe. When they did the auction of the furnishings, they didn't bother with the attic because they couldn't find the key. Remember? Well, I have a spare key and I know how to get up there from the old servant's entrance, so I can easily get in and out without being seen."

Tom gasped. "Milo! That's a horrible idea! What if Milo gets caught? Milo could be arrested for trespassing!"

I shrugged. "I don't think that Chief Baker would arrest me. He knows that's been my family home for five generations before me. And technically, until it finishes escrow, it's still mine. Right?"

"Omega please. Milo is well aware that the bank foreclosed on that property after Milo's father died. That is why Milo was unable to retrieve the belongings inside and now must break in like a thief."

I huffed out: "I'm not a thief if I'm taking what already belongs to me! It's not fair that my dad was able to mortgage Nana's house in the first place. But I can live with that, I have to. I just can't handle not being allowed access to my family belongings."

Tom raised an elegant brow and said: "Well, if Milo isn't a thief, then why is Milo sneaking in through the old servant's entrance in the dead of night? Hmm?"

I hunched over and propped my chin on my forearms that were resting on the tabletop as I looked up at my friend with wet eyes. "I don't know, Tom. All I know is that I can't wait for the new owner to take possession, and hope that he or she will allow me to rifle through Nana's stuff. I just want to find an ending to this legal nightmare and this is the easiest way, okay?"

Tom shook his head, his eyes clouded with concern. Still, he reached over and affectionately ruffled my hair. "Okay, Milo. But Tom will come along and be the lookout so that Milo doesn't get arrested."

"No, Tom! I can do it myself. It will be fine." I sat up in consternation. "I'm not dragging you into this little caper of mine, Tom. It's not happening."

"It is happening, because Tom has declared that it will be so. Besides, if Milo does not include Tom? Tom may have to fire off a few strongly worded hints to Ian and Rafe that Milo needs help." The little shit sat back and crossed his arms over his chest, giving me a smug smile like he already knew he'd won.

Okay, yeah. He totally did win, but only because he knows me so well. "Fine, Tom. Have it your way. But make sure you're photo ready in case we get arrested. I mean, you wouldn't want an uggo mug shot on your record, right?" I smirked at him over the rim of my cup as I took a long drink of latte.

"Milo is evil. But never fear, Tom will be ready for any and all photo-ops. Now, tell Tom why this is being put off until tomorrow? Does Milo have *plans* for tonight? Perhaps plans with a certain sexy alpha?" Tom all but purred as he nosed into my private life with zero regrets.

"Yes. I have a date with Rafe tonight. I'm just cooking him dinner at my place, we're not doing anything too exciting." I tapped a finger against my coffee cup while I waited for Tom to explode into a pushy stream of advice. In less than five seconds, Tom was pushing away his cup and giving me directions for how he saw my evening going. This naturally included a little more over-sharing of his sex life than I wanted to hear.

CHAPTER 7
RAFE

"I can't believe how talented you are, Milo. That was an amazing meal." I smiled and leaned back in my chair at his table. The candlelight was reflected in his glasses, obscuring his eyes but adding to the romantic atmosphere. "Can I help you clean up? Or actually, why don't you relax and drink your wine while I clear the table?"

Milo started to argue, but I got up and began clearing the table. I leaned over the table and pressed a kiss to his lips. "Stay," I whispered against his mouth. "Let me do this for you, Milo. It would mean a lot to me."

He nodded. I stole another kiss then went to work. After the table was cleared, I poured Milo another glass of wine and went back into his tiny kitchen. Milo was a clean cook apparently, because other than what we'd used at the table, there were no other dishes or pots to be washed.

I quickly scraped and rinsed the dishes, then topped off the partially loaded dishwasher. I had just dropped in a gel pod of detergent into the dishwasher and closed the door when I realized that I was being watched. After turning the dial to the wash cycle, I stood and wiped my hands on a clean towel.

I swung the towel over my shoulder and slowly turned. Milo rested with one shoulder against the door frame, watching me with hungry eyes. Leaning back against the counter, I crossed my arms over my chest and smiled at him. "See something you like in here, Milo?"

Milo tipped his wineglass up and drained the final few ounces from it. He walked into the room and set the glass near the sink before turning to me. He came over and tugged my wrists until my arms swung down. Stepping into my personal space, he moved my arms to his hips then ran his hands slowly up my arms until they came to a rest around my neck.

He leaned in and inhaled deeply, as if savoring my personal scent before licking a stripe along my neck, over my jaw, and up to my ear. He took a nip at my sensitive lobe before whispering in my ear. "I liked everything that I saw. An alpha that does dishes? That's straight up omega porn, babe."

I chuckled and nuzzled into the collar of his shirt, kissing the bare shoulder inside. I moved my lips along the same route that he'd done on my neck until I reached his ear. I whispered: "I'm glad I did it then. But that wasn't my intention. I just wanted to give you a few moment's rest. You work too much, Milo. And I work too little. It seemed like the right thing to do."

Milo leaned back into my arms that were now clasped around his waist. His eyes searched mine, and he smiled shyly. "That's what makes you a special alpha, Rafe." He leaned in and kissed me softly, before turning in my arms and pulling my hands apart to free himself. He retained his hold on one of my hands though, as he forged through the apartment pulling me along behind him.

Milo paused in the living room, poised halfway between his bedroom door and the couch. Turning, he looked at me hesitantly. I saw the need in his eyes, and the nervous anxiety in his body language. Milo bit into his lower lip as he looked at me. His entire body was practically vibrating with nervous indecision.

I stepped in close and put my arms around him, pulling his chest up against mine. "What's wrong, Milo. Are you trying to decide what you want to do tonight? It's okay, baby. I promise. There's no rush."

Milo looked into my eyes and took a deep breath before saying: "I know there's no rush for you, but there is for me." He took my hand and put it over his tented crotch. "I need you, Rafe, and I'm sick of waiting."

I gulped. Amazed and terrified by his candor, I searched his eyes but only saw the truth of his hunger there. I squeezed his erection through his pants and leaned in for another kiss. I broke away and touched my forehead to his. "Okay, Milo. Let's go to your bed, baby. But we will only do as much or as little as you want, I promise."

Milo tugged my hand, walking backwards as he pulled me into his room. "I have an idea." He winked at me with a little smirk. "Why don't we recreate the big love scene from *Pretty Omega*?"

My head snapped up as he mentioned one of my steamier books. Fuck yeah, I was on board with this plan! I rushed forward and lifted him by the waist, spinning us around carefully in a circle before carrying him over and putting him down on the bed. Milo giggled and kicked off his shoes.

Following his lead, I kicked mine off as well. I watched, transfixed, as he slowly unbuttoned his shirt. The fact that he wasn't trying to be sensual, but that it was just his practical nature, made it that much hotter. After his shirt came off, I stilled his hands that were about to unfasten his pants.

I knelt down in front of his perch at the end of the bed, pushing forward between his thighs. "Don't, baby. I wanna unwrap your package myself. This is better than Christmas morning," I said huskily as I threw him a wink.

Milo blushed, his hands fluttering onto his thighs as if

he didn't quite know where to put them. I slowly reached up and cradled his face with my hands on each cheek. "It's okay, baby. We have time. Let's enjoy this moment, okay?"

He nodded, and I slowly slipped his glasses off. "I'm going to put these aside, so they don't get broken, okay?" He nodded as I got up to put his glasses on the night table.

Coming back over to Milo, I shed my shirt and let it drop on the floor. Pushing my pants down, I stepped out of them and kicked them over by my shirt. I stood in front of Milo, wearing only my black boxer briefs.

Milo looked at me, his eyes slowly giving me the elevator as he drank me in. I reached up and teasingly stroked my Van Dyke goatee as I looked down at him. "Hmm. Now that I have you here, what am I going to do?" I mused aloud, smirking as Milo blushed crimson.

I slowly ran my hands down over my six-pack abs, watching as Milo's eyes followed my every movement. I went back over to him and knelt between his legs. "I'm only teasing, baby. I know exactly what I'm going to do with you."

"What's that?" Milo asked in a raspy voice as I easily unfastened his pants.

"First, I'm going to ask that you stand up." Milo stood on shaky legs, looking down at me with wide eyes. "Now I'm going to finishing opening my present," I said softly as I pulled down his pants and underwear in one smooth move.

Milo held onto my shoulders as he stepped out of his garments. His erect dick bounced in my face, a hint of liquid already oozing from the slit. I reached up and wrapped a gentle hand around it. It was a perfect size, average in length and girth. My hand fit around it like a glove. I leaned forward and licked the moisture from his slit while my hand slowly stroked along his length.

"Oh, my." Milo said softly, his trembling legs shaking visibly. With my free hand, I tapped his hip.

"Sit back down, Milo. I don't want to worry about you falling over. This is about pleasuring you, not injuring you, right?" I smiled easily, hoping to calm his nerves. I'd already figured that Milo had to next to no experience in the bedroom, an idea that his nervous reactions were confirming for me.

Milo nodded nervously and all but collapsed back onto the mattress. I moved in closer, stroking his dick and asking him softly. "Are you sure about this, Milo? I don't want to rush you into anything that you don't want to do."

"I'm sure!" Milo answered quickly. "I'm just nervous. Just, umm, be patient with me?" His eyes focused just to the right of my face, as though he were too shy to meet my eyes.

"I'll be as patient as I need to be, baby. I just want you

to know that you can call quits at any time and I'll just cuddle you instead, okay?" I turned my head and sucked one of his nuts into my mouth. Milo squirmed and let out a soft moan, letting me know that I was on the right track.

I tongued first the one nut, then the other, taking turns rolling them around in my mouth while my hand stroked his length. I moved back up from his tight sac, licking a stripe up his length to his now leaking slit. When I sucked the entire head into my mouth and swirled my tongue around the ridge and slit, Milo fell backward onto the bed limply.

Pushing my heard forward, I took him all the way down to the root. The head of his dick was rubbing against the back of my throat as I began to move up and down. I watched the play of expressions that chased across his face while I sucked, licked, and teased him. He swelled harder in my mouth as his face contorted. He gasped out my name and shot into my mouth.

I swallowed every drop, then pulled off and licked him clean. Milo lay panting as I pushed off my own underwear and crawled up onto the bed over top of him. I crouched over him on hands and knees and leaned over to kiss him. He gasped into my mouth, no doubt tasting the flavor of his release on my tongue.

Breaking the kiss, I asked: "Was that alright?"

Milo smiled dreamily at me. "Yes, but I thought we

would do more stuff though? It seemed a bit one-sided to me."

I tilted my head and closed my eyes when I felt his small hand reach down and tentatively stroke my rock-hard cock. "And what would more stuff entail exactly, baby?"

Milo surged forward and kissed behind my ear, wrapping his arms around my neck to pull me closer. He whispered between kisses, "I was hoping that you would take me and make me yours tonight."

I stilled, forcing myself to breathe and not come on the spot like a horny little schoolboy. "You mean, you want everything tonight?" I gasped as he nibbled on my earlobe. His hot breath against my ear was making me come undone and we hadn't even started yet.

"Yes. I have a condom in the drawer there, if you want it." Milo sounded shy but firm in his desire. I pulled away and stretched over to open his drawer by the bed. Sure enough, there was a small bottle of lube and a few loose condoms in there. I pulled out the lube and a condom.

"I'm not gonna lie, Milo. I'm both shocked and turned on that you have these. I didn't know if you were thinking along these lines just yet." I opened the condom and quickly suited up while I spoke. His eyes were tracking my every movement with utter fascination.

"They, umm, gave those to me a while back when I went for a physical. I just shoved them in the drawer and forgot about them until now." The combination of his shy blush and pupils blown wide with desire was almost my undoing. I squeezed a death grip around the base of my cock, willing myself to hold on.

I stood on my knees, settling between Milo's open thighs. I ran my hands up the back of his silky thighs as I gently pushed them up to his chest. Reaching over, I grabbed the lube that I'd left laying at his side. With a loud snick, I opened the cap and squeezed a generous amount into my hand.

I tossed the bottle to the side and rubbed my hands together to warm it up before I reached down and teased my way into his tight pucker with a single finger. Milo's eyes went wide from the unfamiliar sensation. "It's okay, baby. Just relax," I whispered. "We are in this together, right? I won't hurt you."

He nodded, and I bent over to kiss him as I added a second finger. Milo gasped into my mouth but went pliant beneath my ministrations. Sucking his bottom lip between my teeth, I nipped at him gently while my fingers scissored inside his hole. His eyes fluttered closed as I added a third finger, opening him up while I kissed and nibbled at his lips.

"Please, Rafe. More. Give me more now," Milo moaned against my mouth. He moaned sadly as I removed my fingers. I smiled against his lips as I rubbed my lube covered fingers over my sheathed cock before lining it up with his hole.

I pushed the fat mushroom shaped head against him and went back for another kiss as I gently broke through the tight ring of muscle. Milo tensed but relaxed slowly as I eased deeper inside him while also deepening our kiss. Once I was fully seated, I held still for what seemed like forever and let his body adjust to my girth.

Breaking our kiss, I lifted up onto my knees. Milo's legs went around my waist as he reached up to grip my biceps with both hands. I gripped his hips and slowly pulled out almost completely before slowly gliding back in. It only took a few strokes before Milo was into the rhythm and pushing back against me with each pump of my hips.

"Harder, Rafe. I need to feel you deeper," Milo moaned, his eyes focused directly on me as we rocked against each other. Without pausing, I pushed deeper with my next thrust. Milo gasped with pleasure as I sped up my thrusts. With faster moves of my hips, I began thrusting into him harder.

Gripping his slim hips with a firm grasp, I held him against me as I fucked into his channel with fast, hard strokes. Dripping sweat now, I leaned my head back and let myself go. Lost in the moment, I growled out his name as I felt the familiar tightening in my abdomen. I reached out blindly for his dick, taking it in hand and stroking in rhythm with each thrust of my cock.

Milo screamed out my name as his hole clenched around me. Hugged by that tight channel, my cock burst at the same time that his shaft began pulsing in my hand. I opened my eyes and looked down at him. His flushed face was beautiful as he gritted his teeth and spurted thick ropes of nectar.

My body jerked as my hips rutted mindlessly through my own release. Once I was done, I carefully pulled out and removed the condom. I managed to tie it off and toss it into the bedside waste basket before I flopped down limply beside my omega.

I held out a seemingly boneless arm, and he scooted right up into my embrace. His head rested on my shoulder as I inhaled his spicy pumpkin scent. Glancing over at him, I smiled at the way his normally neat hair plastered wetly against his head. I ran the back of my hand across his cheek as I gazed into his eyes. How this mild-mannered little candy maker had just completely made me come undone was beyond me.

After our breathing leveled out, Milo asked me: "What happens now?" I was confused as to what he meant, but before I could ask, he continued. "That didn't come out right. I don't mean what happens next between us in general. I meant, do we pass out or clean up and pretend that nothing happened."

Fighting back a chuckle, I turned to him with a soft smile. "Well, first of all, I doubt that I would ever be able to pretend that we didn't do that. And as to the rest? I'm pretty sure that if I tried to move right now, you'd have to call 911 to revive me. So, how about we talk?"

He looked surprised at my suggestion but nodded happily. "What should we talk about? I'm pretty sure you already knew that I hadn't exactly done this before, so I have no idea what one says during post-coital snuggling."

I laughed at that. His look of dismay sobered me immediately though, and I leaned over to rub my nose against his. "I'm sorry, baby. It's just that phrase! Post-coital? Please don't hate me for this, but I'm totally gonna have to use that in a book someday."

Milo smacked my gut and snorted indignantly. I laughed all over again as I turned to cuddle him closer. "Oh, Milo. Please don't ever change. And just to let you know? I've never had post-coital snuggling with anyone else in my life, so this is new for me too."

His eyes lit up at my words. He ran his fingers through my damp chest hair and said softly: "Really? I'm glad then. This way we both got to have a night of first times."

I nuzzled his ear and kissed his jaw. "Milo, I'm happy to share every first with you that you have to offer. I just wish that I had a few more firsts to share with you myself."

Milo's hand rested on my chest as he sleepily replied: "It's okay, Rafe. I don't need to be your first. But I sure wouldn't mind being your last."

I listened as his breaths evened out into sleep while my mind raced at his words. Normally, if I'd heard something like that I would have been half way out the door before he'd finished speaking. But with Milo? I not only didn't want to run for the hills, I actually wanted to stay. The idea of him being my forever sounded better than I ever would have imagined it would.

CHAPTER 8

MILO

I was just plating the omelet I'd made him when Rafe entered my kitchen. He stood there blinking in confusion. Biting back a smile, I poured him a cup of coffee and added a bit of cream with two sugars. I carried it over and handed it to him.

He looked down at the coffee then back at me as a smile slowly spread over his face. "You have coffee? Thank you, baby." Rafe leaned over and kissed my cheek. I guided him to the open door that led to the small balcony that ran along the length of the kitchen and dining area side of my apartment.

"Here, babe. Sit down and drink your coffee. I made breakfast. Let me grab our food and I'll be right back to join you." He nodded blankly and took a seat at the small bistro style table that I kept on my balcony.

About halfway through breakfast, Rafe finally came

fully awake. It was amusing to see how he acted in the morning. "So, not a morning person?" I asked with a small laugh as he looked around him in confusion as if seeing the patio area for the first time.

Rafe grinned and took a long drink of coffee. "Nah, not so much. I'm more of a stay up late and sleep until noon type of guy."

I shook my head. "As lovely as that sounds, I'd be out of business if I kept those kinds of hours. There are many days when I'm in the kitchen before sunrise, especially during the holiday season."

He nodded. "I wondered about that. Do you ever bring in extra seasonal help?"

"Oh, hells yes! I could never handle the fall rush without having extra hands on deck to assist me. From mid-October until Christmas I'm pretty much slammed. Other than that, I have my Valentine's Day and Easter rushes. But the fall is definitely when I make most of my money." I bit my lip, thinking about how badly my fall would go if I didn't find my Nana's recipe book tonight.

"What's wrong, Milo?" Rafe's voice cut through my distracted worries. "You went somewhere else just then. Want to talk about it?"

I shook my head. "Not just yet. Once I get everything figured out, I'll tell you all about it. I just need to do a few things first." I took a drink of my coffee and asked him about his plans for the day. It was easier to talk about him than my own troubles.

"Well, I do have one bit of good news." He grinned around the piece of toast that he held to his mouth. After taking a bite, he set it down and reached for his coffee before continuing. "That house that I told you I was looking at here in town? The bank finally accepted my offer a few weeks ago. I'm actually sleeping there tonight."

My jaw dropped in amazement. "That's wonderful news! But, don't you have to wait for escrow?"

Rafe shrugged. "Well, I mean, I guess? But it closes in a few days anyway. I'm not trying to move anything in just yet, but the realty company gave me the key to the lock so that I can go in to measure and shit like that. I figure, I have the key, so why not?"

I chewed my lip thoughtfully. "But won't you get in trouble? Why not just wait?"

"Baby, are you seriously unaware of the cache that comes along with the Smythe name? I don't want to sound like a pompous asshole, but they won't do more than chide me respectfully and shake their heads if they find me in the house before I close escrow. I'm just excited. I can't wait to show you the place, it's a real beauty."

I sighed, thinking of how much he would have loved my family home. But there was no use thinking about that. Dad had made his choices in life, and I had to clean up the financial mess that he'd left behind. Unfortunately, the loss of my family home and the auctioning of our paintings and other various furnishings is what it took to make it all go away.

Now I was left in my cozy little apartment, and I was just fine. I had my candy store, my friends, and now a hot alpha on my arm. What more could I possibly need? "Well, just be careful, Rafe." I said after I realized that I'd gone silent again. "I'm sure you're right about the bank not caring, but I'd hate to see you get in trouble."

"Don't worry, babe. I'll be just fine. There's not any furniture yet, but I'll take my sleeping bag and a backpack with a change of clothes. I figure even roughing it there will be better than listening to another night of Ian and Tom trying to break the mattress in his bedroom." He shuddered with a small laugh as he said that.

"Seriously? Tom didn't tell me that he was going over there all the time. I didn't even know that they were serious about each other." I began stacking our dishes as I took a discrete look at the time. I needed to be a work in another hour, although I did hate to rush off.

"Well, I don't know how serious they are about each other," Rafe laughed. "But they are pretty serious about hooking up about every night of the week. Why do you think I'm rushing to stay in the new place? Trust me, it's not because I'm impatient. I'm just done being an unwilling voyeur into our friends sexcapades."

I giggled as I stood and picked up our dishes. I walked into the kitchen and set them in the sink while I turned to empty the dishwasher. Rafe had come in right behind me though and was already opening it to do exactly that. "Let me give you a hand really quick, Milo. I know you've got to work today. Four hands are better than two, right?"

"Thanks," I said with a smile. "I won't turn down the help, although I'll say again, it is really sexy to see an alpha that does dishes."

Rafe grinned back at me and said: "Milo, if you think this is sexy, then you should see me with a toilet brush." He waggled his eyebrows and continued: "I clean a damn fine toilet, let me tell ya."

I laughed and turned to rinse our breakfast dishes to load in the dishwasher once it was empty. The next hour flew by as Rafe helped me finish in the kitchen before joining me for a shower. That was a whole other experience, showering with a partner. I'd been shy at first, but Rafe had a way of making me relax without even trying. Before I knew it, we were kissing each other good-bye as we went our separate ways.

I fretted on my way to work, wondering if I should have told him about my family financial disaster and how the competitor was trying to steal my Nana's recipe. I knew without asking that Rafe would be there for me. I just really needed to do this on my own.

Hopefully, tonight when I went to the house, I would find the recipe book and that would solve everything. Then I would call Rafe tomorrow and tell him the whole sordid story and show him the recipe book before I called my lawyer. But first, I had to make it through today.

CHAPTER 9
RAFE

I looked around the gracious old manor that would soon belong to me. I imagined Milo at my side, and how rosy a future with the omega would be. Walking through the ground floor, I couldn't shake the weird feeling of being watched. I passed through the surprisingly modern kitchen. The previous owners had spared no expense in the room.

Milo would flip when he saw the wide granite counter tops and the huge six burner stove-top. The double ovens would be perfect for making large meals during the holidays when we'd gather with our friends to celebrate the season. I shook my head, amused at how I was already planning a future with my shy omega.

It seemed natural though. For some reason, I couldn't picture living in this house without Milo. He just belonged here, I could feel it in my bones. I wandered upstairs and poked around the various bedrooms and bathrooms. The small study would make a perfect writer's cave for me.

Again, even as I imagined myself working there, the image of Milo came to mind. I would be sitting at my large wooden desk, engrossed in the scene I was creating on the laptop screen when Milo's hands would rest on my shoulders as he leaned over to see what I'd written before kissing my cheek. He'd gently tell me to wrap it up because dinner would be ready soon.

As I smiled at the image, I looked up to the window and about jumped out of my skin when I saw a plump little old lady reflected there. I spun around to see her smiling at me with sparkling eyes and rosy cheeks. Her whole body was round and soft-looking, like it was made to give hugs and cookies to small children.

Once I found my voice, I said: "I'm sorry. I didn't know anyone else was here right now. I'm Rafe. And you are?"

She chuckled merrily and waved me off. "I'm Agatha, my dear boy. I just wanted to pop in and see how things were in this old place. Forgive me for startling you."

Now that my pulse had slowed to a more normal rate, I smiled easily. "No worries, Ma'am. Did you know the people who used to live here? It's a beautiful old place, right?"

Agatha smiled lovingly as she ran a hand along the chair rail that ran along the lower third of the wall. "It is a beautiful home, yes. But more beautiful are the many happy memories that these walls contain."

I smiled with a mutual affection for the house. After all, I wouldn't be buying it if I didn't love it already. "I bet," I said. "If these walls could talk, right?"

Agatha smiled and said: "You'd be surprised, young man. Now tell me, Rafe. What led you to this house? I assume that you're the new owner?"

I nodded, realizing suddenly that she still hadn't told me how she knew the house or how she'd gotten in. I could have sworn I'd locked the door. Surely the old bird didn't have a key, right?

"Yes, Ma'am. I'm the new owner. I looked all around for a home in the area, but nothing was right until I walked in the door of this beauty. It was like, I knew I was home. Does that make sense?"

Agatha nodded, her head of silver curls bobbing with the movement. "It does. I've always felt the same since the day I first stepped through the front door when I was but a young bride just moved to town. There's a certain peace to this old place."

I turned to look out the window and admire the colorful flower garden that lined the backyard. "How did you say that you knew the former owners again, Ma'am? Were they friends of your husband?"

When there was no response, I turned around to find

myself alone. I shook my head, wondering where the sweet little lady had wandered off to and if I should have made her leave the second I'd seen her. Somehow, it hadn't seemed like the right thing to do though.

I looked around the entire upstairs area, but there was not another living soul on the floor except for me. I took a glance at the door to the attic, but when I went to open it, it was locked. Obviously, she hadn't gone that way then.

After I made my way back downstairs and looked around, I had to accept that she'd ducked out the way she'd come in. Which I soon discovered wasn't the front door, because it was still locked like I thought it was.

The weirdest part was that as I shook my head and went back to exploring the house, I could have sworn that I heard giggling. But that was impossible, because I was once again alone in the house.

I ducked out later in the afternoon to pick up some dinner. The only downside to squatting in what would soon be my own home, was that there was no food or power. The only reason there was running water was apparently because the realty company had wanted working toilets during the open house.

I'd wanted to pop into Sweet Ballz and surprise Milo, but they had already closed for the day. I looked at my watch, surprised to see that it was already a quarter after six. I fired off a text to Milo instead and went to the diner to pick up the deli sandwich that I'd ordered to-go.

When I pulled up to the manor a short time later, I was shocked to see all the lights on inside. What? Lights? Who had turned the power on? And when? As I got out of the car, I could hear lively jazz music playing inside. I scratched my head, wondering if Milo had come over to surprise me. But no, that couldn't be, because I hadn't told him where I lived yet. Although, it was a small town, so it wouldn't be unheard of for him to know where I was moving.

Ian was another viable option, except for the fact that Ian would sooner kiss a girl than listen to jazz. The man had no taste for any music that wasn't played in the clubs. I shook my head as I dug out my keys, excited to see who was waiting to surprise me on my first unofficial night in the new house.

But when I walked inside, the house was dim and silent. I flicked the light switch, thinking that whoever was here was teasing me. Flick, flick. Nothing. There was either no juice to the switch or no light was plugged in because it didn't work. The light of the dying day filtered in through the open curtains, but no other lights were present.

My heart raced as I went from room to room flicking light switches, but nothing worked. I knew there had to be a reasonable explanation, but there was nothing that came to mind. A floorboard creaked overhead, and I restrained myself from calling out. Maybe whoever was here wasn't a friend after all.

And yet. The house still felt peaceful and welcoming, as if I'd come home after a lifetime away. I set my food down on my sleeping bag and rifled through my backpack for a flashlight. I dialed 911 on my cell but didn't hit send. I just wanted the comfort of knowing that it was good to go if needed. I put my phone in my shirt pocket and headed for the staircase.

I slowly climbed the stairs, keeping to the wall so as not to accidentally step on any creaky boards. Once I reached the upstairs level, I cased the floor like a SWAT team member as I carefully edged around corners before shining my light into each room. I went over the entire floor, but nothing was to be found.

I stopped near the door to the attic and scratched my head again. On a whim, I tried the knob. It turned easily in my hand, which surprised me to no end since the realty agent had told me that no known keys existed to open that door. And it had been locked just a few hours ago. Hadn't it? As I slowly swung it open, a blast of cold air rushed at my face, as if I were facing into a fan.

My pulse raced as a stream of cold sweat ran down my spine. Shaking my head at my silly notions, I went up the narrow staircase. It was so cold, that I could see my breath every time that I exhaled. Weird. Maybe a window was open up here? Even then though, it shouldn't be this cold in September. Especially in an upstairs attic. I mean, everyone knows that heat rises.

At the top, I looked around at the piles of things from yesteryear. There was nobody here but me, so I was free to explore. An old seamstress dummy stood near the window with a half-finished dress pinned to it. The faint light coming in the window showed the faded gingham fabric that was held together with brightly colored pins.

I stopped to look at a nifty old croquet set that sat just past the door in a wooden caddy. It looked to be complete. "Huh," I said aloud as I squatted in front of the caddy and ran a hand over a smooth wooden mallet. "I'll have to take you downstairs when I have Milo over. I bet he'd get a kick out of playing croquet with me. I'll just make sure that he knows I have permanent dibs on the red ball."

When I said Milo's name, the arctic air seemed to warm up by several degrees. I guess even my house liked the sound of his name. I know I sure as hell did. Standing again, I continued my explorations. There was a plethora of old toys and rows of dusty books along one side of the room. The stack of paintings against the wall near the chimney caught my eye, but I decided to wait until daylight to look them over.

The light was dying, and I didn't want to stay up here

in this weird attic armed only with a flashlight. I took a long look around the room. My gaze was drawn to an old wardrobe cabinet tucked into a corner with a huge wooden chest sitting next to it. I went over to give it a quick look. I couldn't explain it, but I was simply drawn to it with a magnetic pull.

I ran my hand over the smooth wood, admiring the craftsmanship of whoever had built this beautiful piece of furniture. The large chest next to it was crafted of the same wood. Obviously the two belonged together. I patted the top of the chest, thinking ahead to where it might fit into my home when I began furnishing it.

The sudden clatter of balls and wood falling against the wooden floor made me jump at least a foot in the air. I clutched my chest, as if trying to keep my heart from jumping out through my skin. I drew in a shaky breath and decided that my exploration was done. I quickly made my way to the stairs. When I got near, I saw the croquet caddy laying on its side, with the mallets and balls strewn all around it.

I didn't stop to wonder how the fuck the heavy caddy had fallen over with nobody there to push it. Nope. I didn't even stop to think about thinking about it. Instead, I dodged my way through the balls, and ran down the flight of stairs like my ass was on fire. I thought that I heard a faint giggling sound, and a thunking behind me on the stairs. I quickly propelled myself through the door.

As I went to shut the door, I noticed a lone croquet ball sitting on the bottom step. Ah. The source of the noise. I shut the door and made my way downstairs. I must have kicked the ball accidentally as I was making my escape. That was the only logical explanation.

The fact that the ball I'd seen on the stair was the coveted red one was something that I dared not consider thinking about tonight. At least, not until I had a stronger drink on hand than the bottled water that I'd brought with me for tonight.

CHAPTER 10

MILO

"I'm serious, Tom." We were standing outside my old family home after we'd made our way in from the neighbor's yard that backed up to the old house. "You need to wait out here. I'm just slipping in and back out again. You just came to stand watch, remember?"

"Yes, well. That was before Tom realized that standing watch meant standing out here in the scary empty yard. Tom does not do scary, Milo! Tom promises not to touch anything, but Milo has to let Tom come inside too." His normal bravado wasn't there. When I saw his trembling lip, I realized that Tom was genuinely scared.

"Tom," I hissed into the quiet night. "You grew up playing in this yard with me! There's not an inch of this property that either of us have yet to explore. Come on, man. You know that there's nothing to be afraid of here."

"Milo. Tom knows that the house is not scary. What is scary are random people that hang around empty properties. How do we know that we're not the only ones here?"

I sighed. Obviously, there was no point in arguing. As usual, Tom was going to get his way, because I needed to get this done. "Fine. But no talking, no touching, and no wandering off. You will be closer to me than my shadow until we're out of here, got me? I'm serious, Tom. This is my livelihood we're talking about here. We don't know who's buying this house, so I'm not guaranteed a second shot at finding this recipe book."

Tom nodded with a contrite expression. "Tom will behave. Milo can trust Tom, m'kay? Tom promises. Scout's honor."

I grinned. "Everyone knows that Tom was never a scout, but that's good enough for me. Let's go get this over with, okay?" Tom nodded eagerly, happy that I was letting him come inside with me.

Using my old house key, I let us in the side entrance that opened into a small potting room behind the kitchen. I jerked my chin at Tom to enter ahead of me, then quietly slipped in behind him. I pulled the door shut and pointed toward the secret panel for the servant stairs that ran up the wall behind the kitchen.

My fingers easily found the hidden mechanism that made the panel silently glide open for us. Once we were both inside, I closed it behind us and turned on my flashlight. There were no windows in this old private stairwell, so we were safe to use the lights.

The entire house was accessible from the servant stairs. This was a throwback from the days when my ancestors depended on their staff to do everything but wipe their butts. Heck, some of the old jerks had probably even expected help with that. Shaking my head, I tiptoed up the stairs with Tom on my heels.

There was no reason to be quiet now that we were safely inside, I just felt more respectful being quiet since it was no longer my family home. We got to the second floor, and I ignored the sliding panel that would take us onto that floor. Instead, I took the turn in the landing to climb the rest of the stairs that led to the attic.

The panel up top opened a section of wall to the far left of the main staircase that led here from the second floor. I tiptoed through the old toys and rows of books, using the beam of my flashlight to guide me. Tom stayed true to his word and was practically glued to me as he walked a half step behind me. I stopped for a moment and swung my light around the area.

My heart caught as my eyes roamed over the old treasures. Over by the window was the dress that Nana had been sewing when she died. We'd left the dress intact on the old dummy because it felt wrong to toss it. I smiled sadly at it, highlighted there in the moonlit window.

I could almost smell Nana's lilac perfume. Being here, surrounded by her things, made me miss her so much that my throat hurt. Swallowing my grief, I trained the light over the piles until I found the cabinet that I'd been looking for over in the far corner.

"Okay," I whispered. "The cabinet is across the room in the corner, if I remember right, the trunk is right beside it. Either stand right here or follow me, but let's get this over with so we can get out of here."

"Tom agrees. But Milo is crazy if he thinks that Tom is staying by himself in this creepy old attic."

I snorted but led the way. We'd only made a few steps when there was a loud crash right before Tom let out a high-pitched, spine curling scream and fell flat on his ass. I shined the light over him and saw that he was lying flat on his back surrounded by Grampa's old croquet set.

What the hell? Why wasn't it all put away in the caddy? That was a lethal accident just waiting to happen. I kicked a couple balls to the side as I made my way over to where Tom lay splayed in the middle of it all. I bit back a grin when I noticed how artfully he had fallen.

Only Tom would manage to artfully land on his ass when tripping over balls and mallets in a deserted house. Hmm. There was a joke somewhere in that, but this was definitely not the time to go there.

I bent to help Tom when the sound of pounding feet came running up the stairs. I froze as the light from a flashlight beam highlighted the two of us. My hand came up instinctively to block my eyes. I couldn't see who held the light, but heard Rafe's voice say: "Milo? What the actual fuck?"

CHAPTER 11

RAFE

I'd finally managed to calm my shit from the craziness in the attic and had eaten my sandwich. I was spread out my sleeping bag in one of the sitting rooms downstairs and nestled in for the night. Milo hadn't responded to my text from earlier. I wondered if he was okay and hoped that he wasn't sitting at home freaking out about our intimacy of the night before.

I could see a future with Milo. The longer I was in this house, the more I wanted to see him in it with me. I couldn't explain it, but it really felt like this house wouldn't be a true home without Milo in it with me. I sent him one more quick text to say that I was thinking about him, then opened Words with Friends to play my turns on the open games that I had going.

I had just scored sixty-eight points on a triple word with the letter 'x' when I heard a loud crash from upstairs followed by what sounded like a banshee wailing. Without hesitation, I jumped up from my nest on the floor and hightailed it upstairs.

I heard a floorboard creak above my head in the attic. Fuck. Again, with the creepy ass attic? It was moments like this that I hated being an alpha. Alpha's were expected to be brave, but I honestly wasn't feeling it right now.

But, this was about to become my home, so I had to alpha up and investigate. I swung open the door to the attic and ran up the stairs, only stopping to retrieve the red croquet ball on my way up. It wasn't much of a weapon, but at least I had something solid in my hand.

When I shined my light on the intruders, the last person that I ever expected to see was Milo. If I hadn't been so scared, I probably would've smelled his strong pumpkin spice scent from downstairs. I wasn't exactly paying attention to those little details at the moment though.

"Rafe! Thank God it's you! Wait. What are you doing here?" Milo stopped then, and looked at me in confusion, as if I were the one that was out of place.

"What am I doing here? What are you doing here? What the fuck, Milo? Is this some kind of gaslight situation where you lure me in with your sweet act and then freak me out with the haunted house schtick? And just so that you two could break in here and rob the joint? Seriously? I don't even know what to think right now!"

My fear had turned to rage, and I wasn't thinking before the words came flying out of my mouth. Milo helped Tom up and handed him a flashlight without bothering to look at me. His rigid stance would have concerned me if I wasn't so fucking pissed off. "Tom, could you please pick up Grampa's croquet set while I talk to Rafe? The caddy is over to the left of the stairs." Tom nodded silently and go to work while Milo turned to me. "Rafe? Could we talk over here, please?"

I was fuming, but I carefully stepped over the croquet shit that Tom was gathering. I paused and handed Tom the red ball I was holding before I made my way over to follow Milo. He was leading me over toward the gorgeous cabinet and trunk in the corner. When we got over there, he stopped in front of the moonlit window. I turned off my flashlight and shoved it in my pocket. I made myself ignore the way that the omega looked as he stood there in front of the moonlit window.

"Okay, Milo. You got me over here, now talk. I need you to explain your presence here tonight in a way that isn't going to piss me off or make me think that you're here to steal from me. I'm feeling more than a little betrayed right now, to be honest." I crossed my arms over my chest and leaned against the wall.

Milo startled at my words. His hands flew to his hips as he leaned forward with outrage. "Betray you? Steal from you? That's ridiculous, Rafe! Are you seriously going to accuse and belittle me right now? Instead of hearing me out? Do you not know me by now? And for your information, if I'd wanted to clean this attic out, I would've done it long before now."

"That reminds me!" I interrupted him as I recalled his words to Tom. "What did you mean by *Grampa's* croquet set? Did your family used to live here or something?" I was angry, but still needed answers. Too many weird happenings and coincidences had me on high alert.

Milo sighed and pulled off his glasses to wipe them on his shirt. I refused to smile at this habit of his that he did when stressed. "Or something is more like it, Rafe. This was my family's home, from the day it was built until about six months ago. Remember when I told you that I came from one of the town's founding families? Well, this was our home."

Milo rolled his head back and huffed out a breath. "It's a long story, but basically, my dad took out a mortgage on this house after a string of bad investments. When he died, I lost everything. I had no idea what kind of hole he'd dug, and no way to save the family home. Everything else was auctioned off. The only reason this stuff is still here is because they didn't know where Nana hid the key."

"Let me guess, you had it the whole time?" I asked him sarcastically. I was getting more pissed off now as I slowly realized that Milo had to have been behind my earlier terror up here. The idea that he'd seen me run away practically in tears didn't sit well with me.

"No. It's probably stuck in some random drawer or cabinet. Nana had a habit of putting things in safe places. The family joke was that she hid things so safely that not even Nana herself could ever find them again. When she died, my dad and I used the old servant's passage to move her stuff up here. That door you used just now hasn't been used since I was in fifth grade."

"Wait. Back up. Servant's passage? What the hell kind of gothic horror tale have I fallen into here, Milo? You know, I thought we truly had something here. Are you gas-lighting me for real? What was with that shit that you pulled up here earlier? Was that fun for you? Because it sure as hell wasn't for me."

"Rafe. Hand to God, I didn't get here until about fifteen minutes ago. I definitely didn't know that you were here. I had no idea that you were the new owner, or I would've just come to you directly instead of sneaking in here like a sneak-thief. I get how this looks, but I'm honestly just trying to find my Nana's recipe book. This was the only logical place to look."

I rubbed a hand over my face. The more he explained, the more pissed off I was getting because every answer he gave just raised more questions. And if I was being honest with myself, I would have to admit that his mild, nervous manner didn't seem like he was playing me. Still, I couldn't ignore what had happened earlier.

"Okay. Let's set everything else aside for the moment. What are you really doing here, Milo?" I asked calmly.

"Well, technically, I could ask you the same question since we both know that you're not the legal owner yet. But whatever. We both need answers, I suppose." He sighed and gestured toward the beautiful cabinet. "My PBF Bombz are from my Nana's personal recipe. Those are my top selling candy. My entire business relies on those little balls of deliciousness. I have a competitor that copied it and is now trying to say that I stole it from her."

Milo put his glasses back on and stuck his hand in his pockets. He rocked up and down on the balls of his feet as he continued his story.

"That letter you saw in my shop was a cease and desist notice from her attorney. The only proof that will save my business is my Nana's handwritten recipe. It's in her old recipe book, which is up here somewhere. I'm pretty sure it's in the old wardrobe there. I mean, that's where she generally kept her important stuff if I remember right. I wish I'd taken it when she died, but I was just a kid. Who knew I'd need it someday?"

"You expect me to believe that your father just moved her stuff up without even packing it or looking through his mother's things? That's asinine." I heard how rude I sounded, but I was too pissed and betrayed to care. "And why the fuck wouldn't you just tell me about all this before now? Even you have to admit that it sounds suspicions as fuck, Milo. If you honestly were having competitor issues, you have to know that I would have happily helped you. This bullshit was unnecessary."

Milo's mouth clamped shut. Without another word, he skirted around me with the obvious intention of leaving. I grabbed his arm to keep him in place.

"Wait. You're not going anywhere, omega boy. I still want to know how you got in here, and what the fuck you were doing earlier when you tried to fucking gaslight me while I was up here poking around."

Milo looked at me curiously, but before he could respond, another omega burst into our conversation. "Milo did not gaslight Rafe! Milo was at work all day, and with Tom since then! This was Milo's home, and whether the alpha chooses to believe Milo or not does not matter. Facts are facts, you alpha-douche! Now, either let Milo look for Nana's recipe book or let Milo leave. One way or the other, this interaction is done."

I looked from Tom to Milo. With a sick feeling in my stomach, I said words that went against everything that I'd thought I wanted. "You know what? You're right. This is done. Milo, I can't be with someone who keeps thing from me, then lies to me and sneaks around my home in the middle of the night."

Milo sucked in a tremulous breath and pushed his way past Tom. He ignored the stairs and headed for a section of wall behind the toys with Tom on his heels. I followed them to see what the hell they were doing now. Milo touched a section of the wall, and a panel slid open.

My jaw dropped, but I followed them as they thundered down the stairs. We reached a landing area, and Milo spoke without looking at me as he pointed to a mechanism on the wall. "This will let you onto the second floor if you push it."

He then turned and went down the stairs to the ground floor. When he reached the bottom, he used another mechanism that made another panel open. We ended up in the small potting room that stood off the kitchen. Milo opened the door that led outside and stepped through it.

Without a word to me, Milo passed something to Tom. "Give this to the new owner. This isn't my home anymore. I won't be needing this now." My heart hurt when I heard the tears in his voice, but there was nothing I could say, or go back and not say, at this point.

Tom turned and glared up at me as he grabbed my hand and regally dropped a key into my palm. "Enjoy the house, alpha. And enjoy being alone. Rafe just lost the best thing that ever could have happened to that stiff alpha ass. Congrats on being an ass."

With that, Tom turned on his heel and stalked off into the night in the direction that Milo had gone. I sighed heavily and turned to go back inside. Right as I stepped toward the door, it slammed itself forcefully in my face. I turned the knob, but it was locked tight.

I rolled my eyes at the way this fucked up night was going as I inserted the key that Milo had given me into the lock. The door opened easily enough, and I went back inside. I made sure the door was locked behind me before I made my way to the sleeping bag. Tom had right about one thing. I'd just lost the best thing that had ever happened to me. And I'd never felt more alone in my life.

CHAPTER 12

MILO

I stumbled into the passenger seat of Tom's car, grateful that he'd been the one to drive tonight. After fastening the seat belt, I wrapped my arms around my ribs and held on tight. Tears were streaming down my face, but I barely noticed them except for the way my glasses fogged. My heart was torn in two, my business was definitely going to fail, and I'd given myself to an alpha that wouldn't even listen when I tried to speak.

The driver's door opened, and Tom slid into his seat. He took one look at me, then started the car. Thankfully, he didn't speak, but just drove the damn car. Right now, I knew that speech would be impossible. Tom reached over with one hand and squeezed my knee. The silent show of support broke the dam. My body was wracked with sobs and I couldn't catch a breath.

A few minutes later, Tom was pulling into his own driveway. I sat there, lost in my grief while he got out. Seconds later, my door opened. Tom reached over and released the seat belt before pulling me forcibly from the car. I came out of my fugue long enough to wonder at the secret strength that he hid in that twinkie little body.

He steered me toward the front door, stopping long enough to unlock it before shoving me inside. I found myself being shuttled onto his couch. My shoes went flying and then a fuzzy blanket was being pulled up around my shoulders. Tom brushed my hair back and removed my glasses. He folded them and carefully set them on the coffee table.

In an uncharacteristically husky voice, Tom said: "Stay here. Tom is going for tea and snacks. All of the snacks." He leaned over and dropped a kiss on my cheek before quickly leaving the room.

I closed my eyes and curled up into a little ball on the couch. I huddled there, with my feet pulled up and my side against the back. I clenched the blanket in my fists and hid my face in the upholstery. There was a high-pitched wailing sound in the room, and it took a long time for me to realize that it was coming from me.

Sometime later, I heard the clatter of teacups being set on the coffee table and the rustling of paper and plastic. I didn't have the energy to turn my head. Tom shoved at my shoulders. "Scoot down, Milo. Make room for

Papa Tom." I obediently scooted forward as Tom climbed over the arm of the couch and wedged himself in behind me.

After a bit of finagling, Tom managed to get his legs stretched out on either side of me. He pulled me back against his chest and wrapped his arms around me. I leaned into his embrace, resting my head against his shoulder but still staring into the fabric of the couch. The main crying jag had stopped, at this point it was just snot bubbles and hiccups.

"Tom brought tea, cookies, the secret stash of Milo's PBF Bombz, and a pint of Karmel Sutra. Name the poison, and Tom will deliver it." Tom spoke quietly, his hands stroking my arms.

"I j-j-just don't understand, Tom. I tried to explain! B-b-but Rafe wouldn't listen! You were right. I should have told him about my troubles. But why would he act like that, Tom? I know it was wrong to sneak in tonight, but he wasn't supposed to be there either? R-r-right?" I sniffed into the upholstery, trying to make sense of what had just happened back there.

"Rafe was wrong, Milo. Tom knows." His hand came up to brush my hair back. "Tell Tom everything. Tom is sorry that Tom hasn't been there for Milo lately. Tom is here now, though. For as long as Milo needs Tom, Tom will be there."

I cried a little more before I spoke again. "Tom, you've

always been there for me. You're more than my sexy bestie, you're my brother."

Tom's arms tightened around me. "Tom loves Milo. Milo is Tom's brother. Never doubt that. Now, Tom says it's time for the two best men ever born. Mr. Ben and Mr. Jerry. Yes?"

I shrugged as Tom stretched over to the coffee table. I heard the crackle of plastic and then Tom's voice commanding me to open. Obediently, I opened my mouth and a creamy spoonful of Karmel Sutra exploded on my tongue.

We sat there sharing the entire pint while Tom held me. He fed us both, taking turns filling our mouths with the shared spoon and our favorite ice cream. Once the last bite was done, he set the trash and empty spoon down on the coffee table and reached over to collect our now tepid cups of tea.

He held mine in front of me and waited while I wrapped my hands around the mug before retrieving his own. We sat there silently, drinking our tea while we cuddled on the couch. Moments like these are why I put up with Tom's craziness on the daily. He may be a handful, but when I need him, he's always right there.

After the tea was done, I dozed off at some point. Tom must have extricated himself, because when I woke up, I was stretched out alone on the couch covered by the fuzzy blanket. I sat up and blinked my eyes in confusion at the sunlight streaming in through the window.

"Good morning, gorgeous. Tom must warn you, we are not alone. Ian is in the dining room." Tom came bustling in with a warm smile.

I jerked my head toward him as alarm flooded my body. "I need to leave then. I don't want to see him, Tom! He's Ian's friend!"

"Milo needs to breathe. Tom has already spoken to Ian and gotten more details that were previously unknown. Go wash up and join Tom and Ian for breakfast." Tom started to leave the room but turned back and looked me with a hand on his hip. "No. Do not even think of slinking out of here. Milo is a grown ass omega, and Milo will join Tom for breakfast."

I smirked at his imperious tone. The sweet omega from last night was gone, and Tom's other side was back in charge. "Fine. I'll do it. But I don't have to like it, and I'm not promising to be nice. I'm too raw from last night to be friendly. Especially to another alpha that's friends with Rafe." I grumbled but stood and retrieved my glasses before heading for Tom's bathroom.

After I'd relieved my tortured bladder, I stepped over to the sink to wash up. When I caught a glimpse of myself in the mirror, it almost sent me screaming from the room. My eyes were swollen and puffy. My cheeks were splotchy and complexion pale. I shouldn't have put on my glasses, then maybe I wouldn't be able to see how shitty that I actually looked. With a sigh, I turned and left the room.

Ian and Tom were laughing at something when I walked in, but both sobered right up when they looked up to see me there. I kept my head down and pulled out a chair. Tom pushed a cup of coffee in front of me, which I gratefully accepted.

They talked in hushed tones about nothing in particular while I sipped at my java and wished the floor would open up enough to swallow me whole. While they talked, Tom had managed to plate some food that he set in front of me. I didn't have much of an appetite, but gamely took a bite of cubed cantaloupe.

I politely ate while they continued to talk as though I weren't sitting there looking like something that a cat had barfed up and pretty much raining on their parade with my gloomy mood.

Ian turned to me after I'd wiped my mouth with the linen napkin that had appeared next to my plate at some point. "I'm sorry about what happened, Milo. If it helps, Rafe is miserable as hell today too."

My eyes slid toward him, but I didn't speak. Instead, I took a drink of coffee and tried to find my mental safe space. Tom spoke up then. "Milo. Is Nana's house haunted? Ian just told Tom an intriguing story about why Rafe thought Milo was pulling a gaslight on Rafe."

"What? That house isn't haunted! I don't care what the neighbor's used to say about lights coming on when we weren't there. Let me guess, someone told him about the supposed jazz music that people claim blasts from the parlor when nobody's home?"

Ian looked at me in shock. "Seriously? Other people have witnessed that shit too? Holy shit. Rafe is gonna shit bricks!"

I tilted my head and looked at him through narrowed eyes. "What do you mean by witnessed it too? I think it's just urban legend, made up by people who were jealous of my family. I never experienced anything weird there. That place is peaceful. It's, well, it's home. Okay?"

Tom was shaking his head. "No, Milo. Think! Remember when Tom and Milo snuck out to spy on the college boys next door that summer?"

I grinned. "Tom. I'm pretty sure that was my dad busting us. Why would a ghost want to out us for being a couple of horny stalkers?"

Ian looked at us questioningly, so I explained. "It was right after junior year. My dad was in bed, and we were having a sleepover. Tom was looking through my telescope and saw the neighbor's son skinny dipping with his friends. They were college aged, and totally out of our league."

Tom giggled at the memory as I paused to take a sip of

coffee. "Anyway, we had it all planned. Tom was going to video them with his phone through the fence so that we could watch it back later. All we needed was to get close enough to get decent video footage. We slipped downstairs through the old servant's passage and went out back. We'd only gotten, like, twenty feet from the door when the exterior lights all came on. We were highlighted there like a spotlight was trained on us, while every dog in the neighborhood started barking and howling for no damn reason."

Tom was laughing so hard at this point. I shook my head with a grin and finished. "My dad opened his bedroom window and looked down to see what was going on. When he saw us there, and the lights over the fence where the alpha boys were partying, he just glared at us. He ordered me to get back inside and that was that."

"Yes," Tom added, "but like Tom has always maintained. Milo's dad didn't move fast enough to have turned on the lights that are located in the potting room, and then been upstairs just seconds later to hang out the window. It isn't physically possible. Milo was just too afraid of Milo's dad to listen to Tom when Tom questioned it."

I shrugged. "Well, if there's a ghost or two in the house, I never saw them. And that isn't enough to convince me. Sorry."

Ian grinned and said: "Would you like the counter solution any better?"

At my curious look, Ian said: "Maybe your dad had a guest over that he didn't want you to know about."

"Ewww!" Tom's nose wrinkled as a look of distaste covered his elfin face. "Ian needs to see a picture of Milo's dad before making that comment."

Laughing, I nodded in agreement. "Seriously, Ian. Tom's got a point. I'd sooner believe in ghosts than my dad getting lucky. He was a rich alpha, but he was not only unattractive, he was also a dick."

Ian shrugged. "Why do you think they call those kind of men sugar-daddies? They don't need looks or personality if they've got enough cash."

That hit too close to home, as I remembered the many charges on my father's overextended credit cards for flowers, hotels, and expensive dinners in the city. Tom noticed my face darken and reached over to squeeze my hand.

"Ian is right, but Tom still says ghost for that night. If there had been another man in the house, Tom would have smelled him. Milo knows that Tom never misses a random man on the premises."

I sighed sadly and looked over at Ian. "What happened in the attic? Rafe said something about the attic. Did that have something to do with his attitude?"

Ian explained what Rafe had told him, and I understood better why Rafe had just accused me of gaslighting him. An alpha like Rafe wouldn't want to have anyone, but especially the omega that he was dating, see him running scared. But still. That didn't give him the right to treat me like he had.

"I get it, Ian. I would've been freaked out too. I mean, I'm sure there's some sort of rational explanation. There has to be. But it wasn't me. And I don't appreciate Rafe just accusing me of being a thief. All I wanted was a handwritten book of family recipes! I told him that! Especially after we...well...let's just say that we'd grown close."

Ian's knowing expression made me blush. Tom looked back and forth between us with glee. "No! Milo finally lost his cherry? Really? And Milo didn't tell Tom!"

I groaned and held a hand up to Tom. "Not right now, Tom. I can't. Okay? Maybe someday, but right now, I have too many other things to deal with first. Mainly, Auntie G's and how I'm gonna prove that the bitch stole my recipe."

Ian looked at me with regret and said: "Umm, Milo? In the interest of full disclosure, I should also tell you that Rafe recognized the letterhead on that notice you received. It's from my dad's firm. So, yeah. I mean, I'm not gonna do anything to screw up your case, but you should definitely know that before you say anything else."

I stood up from the table and tucked in my chair. I looked at them both and spoke calmly. "Ian, I'm sorry, but I'm out. Tom, thank you for last night, but I need to be alone right now. I'll call you later."

I didn't give them a chance to respond. I rushed through the living room, pausing long enough to retrieve my shoes, and let myself out for the short walk home.

CHAPTER 13

RAFE

SIX WEEKS LATER

I frowned as I walked into my office and saw the now familiar red ball sitting on my desk. I went over and sat down in my chair. I reached over and picked up the ball, rolling it around in my hand while I wondered what the hell I was going to do.

Ever since I'd taken legal possession of the house and started to move in, I'd been haunted by that fucking ball. It would be on my nightstand when I woke up in the morning, on my desk whenever I went in for a writing session, and once it had even appeared on top of the TV while I was watching porn.

Well, I wasn't really watching the porn so much as thinking about Milo while two men grunted in the background. I'd looked up from my flaccid cock in frustration, only to see that damned red ball sitting on top of the TV. I could have sworn it hadn't been there when I'd sat down, but who the hell knew anymore.

I'd accused Milo of gaslighting me, but short of someone living in the walls, that was impossible now. I'd changed the locks, installed locks on every window, and even put in a security alarm. But I still kept having weird, inexplicable happenings.

I still hadn't bothered to furnish the house yet. I had a bedroom suite in my room, a desk in the office, and a basic living room set-up with a TV in one of the smaller parlors downstairs. Other than that, the place was still as empty as the day I'd first seen it. Well, except for me and the fucking red ball.

I just didn't have the heart to make a home here without Milo. I'd fucked up. And the worst part was that I'd known it while I was doing it but hadn't calmed my shit down and reined in my temper before I'd destroyed my chance at forever.

The ball wasn't the only thing either. I'd kicked off my favorite slippers one night in front of the couch and dozed off while watching TV. But when I woke up, only one was there. I'd torn the room apart, but the other slipper was nowhere to be seen. And it wasn't anywhere else in the house either. I'd begrudgingly put the lone slipper on the shelf under the TV stand in case the other one showed up at some point. But it had been a month, and I was still being mocked every time I watched TV and the damn slipper sat there looking at me.

I'd woken up more than once to hear the faint strains of

jazz playing but could never find the source. Lights would be on in rooms that I could have sworn I'd turned them off in, and that damned door to the attic? Sometimes it was locked, other times it wasn't. More than once I'd smelled delicious scents coming from the kitchen. But it was always cold, bare, and unused the few times that I'd dared to follow my nose in to investigate the scent. At night, I would sometimes hear a floorboard creak overhead, as if someone were walking around up in the attic.

I was *thisclose* to losing my damn mind. But yet, the overwhelming atmosphere of the house was still peaceful. I felt like it could truly be my forever home, but it wouldn't be because something was missing. Well, someone. That ship had sailed though. After what I'd said to him, there was no way that Milo would ever give me another chance.

And then there was Agatha. I hadn't had the heart to ask her where she lived or how she kept getting in. But at least once every couple of days, she would randomly walk into a room I was in to shoot the breeze as though she belonged there. It would be downright spooky if she wasn't such a sweet old lady. And given how lonely I was, I found myself enjoying her random visits.

Ian had suggested that I adopt a dog. It was tempting, just for the company alone. But I was afraid of how an animal might react in this weird old house that I loved so much. At night, I dreamed of running in the yard with a floppy eared mutt while Milo chased us. There was a little one toddling around with Milo, but I always woke up before I could see him too closely.

As if I'd conjured her with my pondering, Agatha came walking briskly into my office. She carried a dusty book in her arm, a cobweb waving from the top of it as she moved into the room.

"Hello, son. How are you today? Did you get much writing done this morning?" She was always interested in my writing, although I couldn't imagine how she knew about my secret profession.

I shrugged. "I haven't really gotten started yet, Aggie. What are you up to today?" At some point, she'd insisted I call her by the pet name. It was familiar to me now, as familiar as her heady lilac perfume.

"Oh, this and that. I'm never really up to much. That's grumpy husband of mine sees to that, I'm afraid." She smiled gently, knowing as well as I did that no man would ever boss this lady around and live to tell about it.

"What do you have there, Aggie? It looks like you dug it out of a musty old attic or something." I nodded toward the old book she cradled in her arm.

"Well, I have a job for you. I cannot stand by while that sweet boy is pushed out of business by a thieving harpy." She walked closer and set the book down in front of me. Goosebumps broke out all over my body as

I read the title. *Personal Recipes* was handwritten on the cover in faded ink.

I sucked in a breath. "Is that...?" She nodded. "You have to mend fences with him, Rafe. It's time, and soon he will need you. Now. I'm not supposed to interfere, but this is important so I'm bending rules a bit. My sweet boy only has until tomorrow to prove his claim. You need to get up and take this to him. Today."

I paled as I pushed my chair back to put distance between me and the proof of Milo's claim. "You don't understand, Aggie. I said awful things to him in a heated moment that I can never take back." I rubbed a hand over my face, my eyes stinging with unshed tears. "He will never forgive me. Trust me on that."

Aggie smiled gently at me. "Son, the only thing that I've learned during my time on this earth is that forgiveness can't be received unless an apology is given. And Rafe? I know all about the things that you said to him, and how both of your hearts were broken that night. Trust an old woman on this though. No heart has ever been broken that can't be mended with a true apology and a willingness to change."

"But what if I'm too afraid to apologize? I don't dare show my face around him. No, Aggie. I'm sorry, but I just can't do it." Even as I spoke, I remembered my dreams of Milo and a toddling child. Wouldn't happiness like that be worth groveling for?

"It would, Rafe. You go and grovel. Throw your alpha butt down at his feet and beg him to give you another chance. Neither of you will ever find the same happiness with another that you will together." She tapped a gnarled finger to her wrinkled brow. "I know things, son. Trust Aggie on this one, hmm? But you must go now. Today."

I was confused for a second, wondering if she'd read my mind or if I'd spoken aloud about my dream. When I looked up to ask, she was gone again. Only the heady lilac fragrance and the dusty old book remained as proof that she'd been there. I rolled the ball around in my hand a few more times, as I weighed the pros and cons. Then as if she were still in the room, I heard Aggie's voice whisper in my ear: "*Just go to him.*"

CHAPTER 14

MILO

I had just finished packing up the last box of PBF Bombz for a large order, when Tom came flouncing through the swinging door. Kent hadn't been able to work today, so I'd had to beg Tom to fill in. It didn't matter. Soon, I wouldn't be able to afford hired help anyway. I'd be lucky to pay myself a wage after I lost the rights to Nana's recipe.

"Milo. Listen to Tom. It's important." He stood there with a hand cocked on his tilted hip, waiting to get my full attention before he continued. "Milo has a visitor. No matter how much that Milo may wish to hide, Tom is sending Rafe back to see Milo. Tom just wanted to give Milo a moment to prepare."

"What? No! It's been six weeks, Tom! He could have texted, called, come by my apartment, or even sent a message by carrier pigeon! He couldn't be bothered to come crawling with an apology before now? Fuck him.

No. I won't see him." My heart raced with excitement though. The thought of seeing my alpha was too thrilling. Wait. No. Strike that. He's not my alpha. He'd proven that, hadn't he? I turned my back to Tom to hide the emotion that I knew was easy to read on my face.

A familiar voice replied: "I can crawl if you want me to, and I will if it means that you'll give me a chance to apologize. But first, let me give you this so that you can save your business."

I spun around to see Rafe standing there holding my Nana's recipe book in his outstretched hands. Tears filled my eyes as I raced over to accept the enormous gift that he had brought me. I traced my fingertips over her familiar, spidery handwriting. The tears flowed as I hugged it to my chest. Not because I was going to be able to save my business and protect a usurper from stealing my Nana's recipe, but because I was holding a piece of Nana in my arms.

Rafe held his arms out, as if wanting to hug me but too ashamed to try. Fuck it. I threw myself into his arms, crying against his shoulder. Crying for my beloved Nana. Crying with happiness for my business. Crying for Rafe and how much I'd missed him. My emotions were all over the place, and it was several minutes before I calmed down.

Rafe was running his hand up and down the length of my spine, murmuring in my ear. "It's okay, Milo. I'm here now. I'm so sorry that I was just an unforgivable ass. Don't cry, baby. Everything will be okay."

I sniffed and pulled away. Looking up at him, I knew that my vulnerability was written all over my face but screw it. I was past worrying about what people thought of me. If there was a chance for us to reconcile, I was going to grab it with both hands and not let go.

"Do you mean that, Rafe?" My voice was raspy and rough. "Is there a chance of us finding a way back to each other after all this time and the words that were said?"

He looked at me, his soul laid bare. I could see the heartbreak in his eyes, and the desire for forgiveness. "Yes, Milo. I mean it. I'm sorrier than words can ever say. But if you accept my apology, and forgive me, then I will spend the rest of time proving to you how much I care. I didn't know what I had until I lost it." He stopped, looking to the side as he chuckled bitterly. "Well, not so much lost it as threw it away like it didn't matter."

He looked back at me then and took a step closer to me. "But you do matter, Milo. In this entire world, I don't think that anything matters as much as you do. Can you find it in your heart to forgive me? To give us another chance?"

I opened my mouth to say *Yes, Yes, All of the Yes!* when a wave a nausea came over me. I thrust Nana's book into Rafe's hands and raced for the bathroom that was just off the kitchen. I dropped to my knees as I made it through the door and slid from the momentum over to the toilet like I was hitting home base.

I bent over and puked my guts out. I could smell Rafe's familiar scent standing in the doorway, but when I turned to look at him another wave hit. I turned back and bent back over the toilet. After I finally finished puking, I scooted back until I hit the wall. I looked up at a very worried Rafe and said: "Yes. I forgive you. That's what I was about to say when the nausea hit again."

"Again?" Rafe's eyebrow flicked up as his worried eyes roamed my face. "How long has this been happening?"

"Milo has been getting sick the past couple weeks." Tom squeezed around Rafe and grabbed a paper towel. He ran it under the sink, and then passed it to me to wipe my mouth. "Tom has begged Milo to see the doctor, but Milo refuses."

"Because it only happens once or twice a day, Tom. It's no biggie. It's probably just stress or something." Even I wasn't buying that one, but I didn't have time to worry about my health right now. First, I had to save my shop.

"I disagree." Rafe said calmly as he tapped the screen on his phone. "Your health comes first, Milo. It's very much a biggie. If you're not healthy, nothing else matters. Now, let's get you to the doctor."

I started to refuse, but Tom was already talking on his phone. "Yes, thank you Stacy. Yes, this is about Milo again. 2:30? He'll be there." I clenched my jaw and tried to interrupt, but Tom just swept out of the room to complete the call.

Rafe's phone pinged. He looked at the screen. "That's Ian. He's on his way over. He will take the recipe book to your attorney's office, while I take you to the doctor. Tom can be trusted to watch your shop for an hour or so, right?"

"What?" I screeched, unable to stop myself. "Ian's father is opposing counsel, Rafe! I can't involve him!"

Tom came back in. "Is it because Milo doesn't trust Ian, or because Milo doesn't wish to cause problems for Ian?"

"I trust Ian, Tom. I do." And I did. Over the past six weeks, he'd shown himself to be a true friend while he and Tom continued their flirtatious little mating dance. "But I can't involve him. That's his father, you know?"

Rafe smiled kindly. "Trust me, babe. There's no love lost there. Ian will be happy to help. He hates corporate greed, in case you haven't had a chance to hear him on the subject yet."

I grinned. It was impossible to know Ian without knowing his anti-corporate views and how he rooted for small business. "Okay. I'm guessing that I don't have a choice anyway, so let's just do it."

"Attaboy, Milo. Tom has trained Milo well." Tom tapped his phone and turned to Rafe. "Tom sent the deets to Rafe's phone. The doctor will see Milo this afternoon at 2:30, in case Rafe didn't hear Tom's call."

"Tom," I asked suddenly. "How did Stacy at Doctor Andrews office know that I needed to be seen?"

"Duh." Tom smirked at me. "Tom has been in conversation with Stacy several times already. There are three things to rule out, based on Milo's symptoms."

"Do I want to know?" I asked hesitantly.

"Well, knowledge is power." Tom shrugged. "Milo could have an ulcer. Milo could have had food poisoning, but it has gone on too long. Milo could have cancer or a stomach problem like GERD. It could be stress, but not likely. Or," Tom dramatically paused for effect. "Milo could be pregnant."

"Well, I know it's not the last one, and I hope it's not cancer. So, I guess I root for GERD?" I laughed humorlessly.

Tom shrugged. "Is Milo sure it's not the last one? I mean, you did have sex, right?" He looked at Rafe's blank face and back to mine with a wicked gleam in his eye.

"Tom. Stop teasing, Rafe. If you must know, we used a condom. Besides, it was just the once and it was six weeks ago!"

Tom smiled wider. "That is the correct amount of time according to Stacy for Milo to be experiencing morning sickness. Now, who supplied the condom? Did it break?"

Rafe covered his face with both hands and groaned at Tom's nosiness. "Tom, you are embarrassing the alpha. Chill out with that pregnancy shit. Besides, I had condoms. You know, the ones that I got when I got my first omega physical."

Tom looked at me then with complete shock on his face for the first time ever. I'd never seen him so completely floored. When he recovered himself, Tom said with a gasp of horror: "Milo! That was seven years ago! Are you mental? Condoms expire after five years! They teach you that in seventh grade health, for God's sake!"

Hearing Tom slip out of speaking in the third person for the first time in over ten years did more to shock me then the possibility of pregnancy. Tom looked at his watch. "Fuck this shit. It's only 1:15. I'm not waiting another two hours for an answer. I'm going to the pharmacy across the street. Don't move, I'll be right back with a piss test."

Tom left in a rush, as Rafe and I looked at each in stunned silence. After several moments, we both started laughing. The more he laughed, the harder I laughed. We were still laughing five minutes later when Tom came rushing back in.

He pulled a box out the paper bag he was carrying. I was still giggling as he ripped open the box and muttered under his breath about stupid virgins and baby daddies or something along those lines while he read the directions.

He turned and imperiously held out a hand to help me up. Turning to Rafe, he said "Step out, please? This is an omega only zone for the next few minutes."

Rafe huffed. "I don't think so. If he's pregnant, then it's my baby too. That gives me more right to be here than you."

"Fine, Rafe can stay." Tom waved a hand at Rafe as he slipped right back into third person conversation. He took the cap off the white plastic stick he held before thrusting the stick into my hand. "Milo, piss on the end of the stick. Then after three minutes, there will be a plus sign in the window of the stick if Milo is expecting Tom's niece or nephew."

"No." I said firmly. I pointed the stick at first Tom then Rafe. "I don't care if you guys fight over the right to handle my piss coated test after I'm done spraying it, but I do not need an audience to do my part in this fiasco. Now both of you, shoo."

Rafe stepped out without argument, while I had to shove Tom through the door. I shut the door in his face while he was winding up for a classic Tom diva-tantrum. *Nope. Not today, Tommy boy. Not this time.* I locked the door with satisfaction and turned back to the toilet.

I lowered my zipper and pulled out my penis, nervous now that the moment was at hand. It took me a moment to get my stream flowing, since I was so nervous. Once I finally started peeing, I put the tip of the stick in the stream for moment then set it aside while I finished. I put the cap over the piss-soaked test strip, and slowly washed my hands before I opened the door again.

Tom and Rafe were sitting at my big work table, waiting for me to come out. I held up a hand to Tom before he could speak, then held a single finger to my lips. "Ssh. Let's just wait and see. No more arguments, okay?"

Tom nodded reluctantly, and Rafe just patted his thigh in invitation. I happily went over and sat down on his lap while we waited for the test to read the results. Ian came pushing through the doors right then, but before he could say anything, Rafe held out a hand. "Come on over, we're about to find out if Milo is pregnant."

The look on Ian's face was priceless. He recovered quickly and said: "Well done, Rafe. When you make up with your man, you do it up right!"

"Shut up, Ian," I giggled. Rafe reached for the test and held it up for us all to see. I sobered quickly as a feeling of awe settled over me. There in the window was a solid blue plus symbol. Rafe dropped the stick and wrapped his arms around me, burying his face in my neck.

"Well done, alpha." Tom said happily as he rubbed his palms together. "Tom has so much shopping to do!"

Ian looked at us all curiously. "Wait. Does that mean that you guys are seriously going to have a baby?"

I nodded. "I guess Tom suspected it because I've been ralphing so much lately. He made me take a preggo test right before you got here."

Ian staggered over to an empty stool and sat down heavily. He blinked at Rafe and me with a blank look in his eyes. "Damn. Rafe! You're gonna be a dad?"

Rafe looked up then, his chin resting on my shoulder. "Yep. Apparently if you use an expired condom it doesn't do much for birth control."

I giggled then, and everyone else laughed along with me. I would probably be embarrassed about my condom snafu later. But right now, I was too happy to care. I'd always dreamed of having a child. Even if Rafe hadn't come and apologized, I still would have been happy about the baby. And I would have done my best to be a polite co-parent once the baby arrived if we'd stayed apart. The fact that we were together again just made it perfect.

"Wait." I said a few minutes later. "Does this mean that I don't have to go to the doctor now?"

Rafe shook his head against my shoulder. “No. It means that we will be seeing the doctor to confirm the pregnancy and find out what we need to do to take care of you. And see if there’s anything that can be done for your nausea. That didn’t look fun, babe.”

I sighed softly. I looked over at Ian. “And you really don’t mind taking that to my attorney’s office?”

Ian smiled and answered: “It will be my pleasure, Milo. And don’t worry, I’ll make sure that they give me a receipt so that you can get it back later.” He rolled his eyes. “Trust me, I know all about lawyer’s offices.”

CHAPTER 15
RAFE

I checked in on Milo before I headed downstairs to lock up for the night. He was fast asleep in my bed, where he belonged. I wondered how long it would take for me to talk him into moving in with me here. Hopefully before the baby came.

He was a stubborn omega, not that I blamed him after all I'd put him through. Even though we'd gotten back together over three months ago, I could understand if he dragged his feet for a bit. I mean, ours was still a new relationship before the break-up. And since then, we'd been busy with the holiday rush at his store and dealing with his morning sickness.

I was ready for the happily ever after, but I also knew that we needed to take the proper steps to get there. Still. It didn't hurt to look ahead and hope for a future filled with Milo. The lights were all on downstairs.

Even on the Christmas Tree. I went from room to room, methodically turning off the lights.

When I entered the living room, I found Aggie sitting on an old chair near the tree. I'd brought it down from the attic at Milo's request. Apparently, it had been a particular favorite of his Nana's. As I entered the room, her lilac scent hit me with a stronger burst than usual.

I didn't question her odd comings and goings anymore. I'd learned to just enjoy the few moments that I shared with the strange old bird. Although I did wish that she'd show up at some point so that Milo could meet her. He looked at me like I was crazy whenever I mentioned the meddling neighbor that liked to pop by unannounced and let herself in and then dramatically disappear soon after.

"Hey, Aggie. Are you ready for Christmas tomorrow?" I asked, slowly lowering myself to the floor across from her. I inhaled the lovely scent of evergreen that filled the room. It melded beautifully with Aggie's lilac perfume.

She smiled at me, as if just noticing my presence. "You've done well, young man. You and Milo make a sweet couple and will be wonderful fathers. Now you just have to give him a special gift tomorrow. Don't worry, he won't say no."

I looked up at her quizzically. She pointed under the tree. I laughed when I saw the red croquet ball sitting there. A glint of something shiny next to it caught my eye, and I reached over to pick it up.

I held a beautifully crafted silver ring. It was etched with a row of tiny shamrocks and hearts in an alternating pattern. I looked at her questioningly. "Where did this come from, Aggie?"

She smiled. "I would suggest telling Milo that it was in the trunk or cabinet that you both love so much but have yet to remove from the attic." She looked into the lights of the tree, her eyes unfocused as if remembering something. Or someone.

"It belonged to my husband, Miles. After he passed, I wore it around my neck for many years. My son intended to bury it with me, but that's not something that I prefer. That ring is a symbol of a lifetime lived with love, happiness, and peace. It needs to rest on another hand that faces his own lifetime of the same."

She laughed then. "Oh, there were fights. Don't let me tell you otherwise! But the best part about fighting with an Irishman is making up afterwards. Well, I suppose that's true in any marriage. But I was partial to my own grumpy Irishman."

I hadn't realized that her husband had passed. She usually spoke of him in present tense during our random conversations. "I'm sorry that you lost him, Aggie. But I can't take his ring. It wouldn't be right to take it from you. A treasure like this ring belongs with family."

Aggie smiled at me then, her luminous eyes filled with tears. "Oh, sweetheart. That right there is the reason that you can take it from me. Your heart is beautiful, Rafe. You will be a good husband to my Milo. My prayer is that you find as many years of happiness together as I did with my husband."

I bit my lip as I looked down at the ring that I still held in my palm. "You don't think it's too soon? I don't want to rush him."

Aggie laughed then, a booming musical sound that filled my heart. "Oh, Rafe. The boy is already swollen with your child. I think the horse has already left the barn, love." She sobered then, looking at me directly as she spoke.

"When you find love in this life, Rafe, you have to grab it with both fists and hold on tight. Some loves are here for a season, while others are here for a lifetime. I think you already know that Milo is your once in a lifetime love. And he knows it too, don't you think otherwise. Don't let fear keep you from happiness, Rafe. Don't you do it. Life is too short. Grab it by the short and curlies while you have the chance."

"I'm assuming you mean life by that last part, and not Milo?" I asked dryly, with a sassy smirk.

Aggie laughed again. "Oh, yes. You'll do for our Milo,

Rafe. My husband would have definitely approved." She shrugged then. "Or maybe he already does? Who's to say? At any rate. Forgive an old fool for her teasing and pranks. I'm happy that you and Milo have found your way back together. Make sure you give him that gift tomorrow, you hear me?"

I nodded. "Oh, and one more thing." Aggie said suddenly, with a hint of laughter in her voice. "Put on some slippers, son. You'll catch a cold." She laughed as I turned to look mournfully at my lone slipper on the TV stand. My jaw dropped when I saw the complete pair sitting there.

I looked back over at Aggie to ask her about it, but the chair was empty except for that damned red croquet ball. I got up slowly, my brain ready to explode at this point. I went over and pulled on my slippers.

I tucked the ring into my pocket and headed for the hall. With one last look around the room, I shook my head and turned off the lights. As I climbed the stairs, I could have sworn that I heard Aggie's laughter following in my wake.

CHAPTER 16

MILO

I woke up on Christmas morning, and smiled at the sight of Rafe stretched out beside me. Deciding that he needed a special Christmas wake-up, I wiggled down under the covers and took his bare cock in hand.

I pulled back the foreskin before licking the hypersensitive flesh beneath. He grew hard in my hand while I teased him with my tongue. I loosened my jaw and took him deep into my mouth, sucking harder with each jerk of my head. A large hand came down and rested on my hair, as Rafe let out a loud groan.

Smiling, I hummed in the back of my throat as I sucked. His muffled curse was all the encouragement I needed. I rolled his balls in my palm with my free hand, while I used the other to stroke his cock in rhythm with my sucking. In no time at all, his balls were tightening in my hand as his hips erratically jerked against me.

I swallowed every drop that flooded my mouth, savoring the flavor before licking him clean and crawling up to kiss him good morning. I knelt over him, my hands braced on either side of his head.

He looked up at me with a wide smile and shining eyes, "Good morning, baby. That was a hell of a wake-up call."

I smiled back at him as I lowered myself for a kiss. "Good morning, my love. Merry Christmas."

We were mid-kiss when Rafe easily flipped me over onto my back, taking control of the situation. His lips never left mine as his hand roamed down my body. He stroked my baby bump a few times, before moving down to grasp my dick. I was so turned on from the blow job I'd just given him that it only took a few quick strokes of his firm grip before I was shooting spurts of cream across my belly.

Rafe broke our kiss and turned around. He licked me clean. Every. Single. Drop. "Damn, Rafe. I never knew you were such a dirty alpha." I said teasingly. He lifted back up and kissed me again.

After passing a serving of my own nectar to me with his tongue, he pulled back and grinned at me. "Yeah, but you love my dirty alpha ass. Right?" His eyes searched mine, as if looking for an answer.

I smiled lovingly at him, but blushed as I said quietly: "Yeah. I definitely do."

He seemed to get whatever he was looking for with that because his eyes lit up. He hopped up and stood by the bed, holding a hand out to me. "Come on, dirty boy. Let's go get cleaned up before Tom and Ian get here."

I groaned, thinking of all the cooking that still needed to happen. And I also wondered how I was going to break it to Rafe that I'd invited Kent and his older brother to join us for dinner as well. I smiled to myself as I followed Rafe into the shower.

"What are you smiling about, babe?" Rafe asked as he pumped some soap into his hand and began to soap up my chest.

"Umm. I'm just picturing the look on your face when I tell you that I invited Kent and his brother, Christian, to dinner today." Rafe's head jerked up from where he'd been smiling at my baby bump.

"Seriously? That little dumbass is coming here?" Rafe rolled his eyes but leaned in to peck my lips. "That's okay, babe. If they don't have anywhere else to go, then I'm glad that you included them. The holidays can be lonely."

I nodded. "Thanks, hon. I'm glad that you understand. I don't know their story, but I do know that it's just the two of them. Christian is a mechanic, and well, you know Kent already. They're nice kids though. Trust me."

"I do. And hey, maybe the brother has a complete brain

cell, huh?" Rafe grinned as he continued washing my body. It was cute the way he loved to take care of me.

I looked forward to the day when I lived here with him, and we could shower like this every day. But I wasn't about to rush Rafe. He'd let me know when he was ready. I mean, we were having a baby in a few months, so obviously he would ask me at some point in the near future.

After we were bathed and dressed, we went downstairs. I dragged Rafe into the kitchen to help me get the food started. Before long, everything was going according to schedule and we were able to take a break.

Rafe led me into the living room. I was heading to the couch to put my feet up, when I saw the red croquet ball sitting on Nana's chair. I gasped and covered my mouth with both hands as tears filled my eyes.

Rafe pulled me over to the couch. He sat down and pulled me onto his lap sideways so that my legs were stretched out beside him. "Wanna tell me what's going on or is it the pregnant emotions thing again?"

I batted at his chest as I rolled my eyes. Then I put my arm around his neck and leaned into him. "How did you know?" I asked quietly.

"How did I know what? I'm sorry, babe. But I'm totally lost here." Rafe looked at me curiously.

"The red croquet ball! Whenever we played, it was

always my ball! I refused to use any other ball, because I said that the red one was special. My father used to tease me when I was little and hide it to make me pick another color. I'd just go on a treasure hunt until I found it." I smiled at the memory. "He called me his little red ball after that."

"After Father died, we didn't play croquet anymore. But Dad would leave that ball for me to find in random places. He said he wanted me to always remember that I was as special as the red ball, just like Father had always said. My dad told me once that when I grew up, I would find my own red ball of an alpha like he'd found with my father."

Rafe looked at me with a stunned expression. "Baby, I know that you swear that this house isn't haunted but remind me sometime to tell you about my own experiences with that damned red ball." He grinned suddenly as he leaned in for a kiss. He spoke against my lips as he said: "And Milo? You're totally my red ball, babe."

"You're my red ball too, Rafe. But just know, if we ever play croquet? I'm always the red one." I giggled as Rafe nuzzled my neck and his goatee tickled my sensitive skin.

The doorbell rang before we could talk any more. I bounced up to get it. Despite my growing belly, I was still light enough on my feet. Rafe was right behind me as I threw open the door.

"Merry Christmas!" I laughed when I saw that Tom was dressed as a naughty elf. He was wearing red and white candy cane striped tights, green booty shorts, and only a leather harness over his otherwise bare chest. The look was completed by green leather peter pan boots, a jaunty elf hat, and kohl eyeliner.

Rafe shook his head when Tom flounced in and said: "What, no lip gloss?"

Tom turned to Rafe and said: "Tom was wearing the perfect shade of peppermint flavored red gloss, but Ian decided it looked better on an alpha's face."

I looked over at a smiling Ian, whose face was covered in red lip-prints. I nodded speculatively before saying: "Yeah, it kinda does, Tommy-boy."

Ian carried a big Santa bag over his shoulder as we led them in to see our tree. Tom insisted that we all sit down so that he could pass out our gifts. Rafe and I snuggled on the couch, while Ian took the recliner that sat at an angle to the couch.

We had fun opening our gifts while Tom danced around delivering them all. The best gift though was right here around me. My make-shift family and the baby in my belly were all I needed. I thought we'd opened all our gifts when Rafe turned to me and said that he had one more thing to give me.

He turned and knelt down in front of me, gathering my hands in his while he blinked away the suspicious dampness that filled his eyes. Once he was ready, Rafe blew my mind with what he said next.

"I got some good advice from my friend Aggie that I keep telling you about. She told me that there are loves that come into our lives for a season, and then there are forever loves. And when we find our once in a lifetime love, we need to grab it with both fists and never let go." He paused, looking down at our joined hands as he gathered his thoughts before continuing.

He looked back up, stunning me with his emerald green eyes that glowed with love for me. "Milo, you're my once in a lifetime love. I almost lost you once, and I don't ever want to risk that again. Will you marry me, and let me be your forever love too?"

Not gonna lie, I was totally shocked right now. I nodded happily. "Rafe. You already are my forever love. Of course, my answer is yes! I will definitely marry you! And not just so that I can beta-read all your books either," I added with a giggle as he leaned in and pressed his lips tenderly to mine.

He pulled back and dug into his pocket. "I almost forgot! I have a ring! Aggie gave it to me, but I was supposed to lie and say that I found it in our favorite cabinet up in the attic."

I looked at him with confusion as he pulled a familiar ring from his pocket. I lost my breath for a second as the room spun around me. As Rafe was busy sliding the ring onto my finger, I finally found my ability to speak.

"Rafe. I need you to tell me more about this Aggie person. I thought that you were making her up with her mysterious visitations to you when you're here alone, but now I'm starting to freak out, babe." Rafe's face clouded with concern as I started to tremble. Tom had been edging in to congratulate us. He saw my face and grabbed at my hand to see the ring. His already pale face went three shades lighter as he gaped at the ring.

Tom turned to Rafe and said in a reverent voice so soft it was almost a whisper: "Rafe, that's Milo's Grampa Miles' ring. Nana Agatha wore it around her neck until the day she died! Milo's dad was gonna bury it with her, but it got lost somehow."

Rafe's eyes bugged out of his head as he asked incredulously: "Nana *Agatha*? Did her friends call her Aggie?" When I nodded, his eyes fluttered back in his head as he passed out cold.

CHAPTER 17
RAFE

I probably drank way more brandy than necessary on Christmas but forgive me if I needed a little liquid reinforcement after discovering that I'd been befriended by a ghost all this time.

Milo had pulled out his phone after I came to. When I was ready to talk, Milo opened his Facebook page. He'd gone through his pictures, until he found an old family photo of him and his Nana that he'd posted a few years ago for Throwback Thursday. Sure as hell, the happy little woman standing next to the adorable little omega boy was my friend Aggie.

Ian was way less freaked out about the whole thing than I was, and Milo just looked rattled. Tom was uncharacteristically quiet too. Every once in awhile, Tom would stop and look at Milo's ring again. Then he'd shake his head and pour himself another eggnog. I was shocked to realize that I was actually okay with it all, despite my original reaction.

Of course, the brandy probably helped with that. Milo had gathered himself in time to finish dinner before the boys arrived. When the doorbell rang, I was surprised to see a cleaned-up Kent dressed in his Sunday best and carrying a potted poinsettia plant for Milo.

His brother was Kent's opposite. He definitely seemed to have a brain, although he was older by a few years. Maybe poor Kent was just young yet. They both had a hard time keeping their eyes off Tom, much to Ian's irritation. Milo called us all to the table, and everything smelled delicious.

I looked over at Milo after I'd swallowed a bite of his honey glazed ham. "Babe? Would it freak you out if I asked if this is by chance one of your Nana's recipes?" This was one of the things that I'd smelled cooking in the unused kitchen a few months prior.

He nodded hesitantly. "Do I want to know? Is this another haunted Nana story?"

I laughed. "Milo. Relax, baby. But yeah, I smelled this exact thing cooking more than once when I was here alone. But there wasn't anything cooking at the time."

Milo shook his head and blew out a long breath. "Okay, then. Well, that makes sense I guess. Nana made this every Christmas. It was a tradition. That's why I made it today. I mean, it's not my house yet, but it was always served here. I couldn't imagine a Christmas without it."

I swallowed another bite and replied: "Milo, you're pregnant with my kid, and we're engaged now. At this point, it's just a matter of how soon I can move you in here."

Milo grinned. "Well, since you're being haunted by my family, I guess I should just move right in."

Tom choked on whatever he was chewing, while Ian slapped his back and laughed at what Milo had said. Ian looked over at me and said: "Damn, Rafe. I hadn't thought of it that way. What a way to meet the in-laws!"

"Careful with that, Ian. Milo will kill us if we drop his Nana's cabinet!" Milo had officially moved the day after that weird Christmas of revelations. We'd waited through January to do more decorating until after we'd gotten the furniture we wanted for the house. I was finally bringing the cabinet and trunk down from the attic.

Milo was putting them in our master bedroom, where we could both use them. Well, the cabinet anyway. The trunk was planned storage for blankets and pillows. It was amazing how the house was coming together under Milo's practiced eye. We had bought a boatload of new furniture, and he was blending in pieces from the attic to add a piece of himself to our home.

Milo and Tom were waiting in our room to direct where the cabinet would stand. Once it was in place, Tom got busy polishing and waxing it while Milo began the long process of emptying it out.

I stopped and rubbed his shoulders after we'd carried in the trunk. "Baby, if it's too hard to go through your Nana's things, I can help you. It's not as personal to me."

Milo looked at me over his shoulder. "You know what though, Rafe? Now that I've come to terms with you somehow seeing and talking to my dead Nana, I'm actually at peace with it. I mean, I would've loved to see her too. But maybe that's not how it's supposed to work?" He shrugged. "Anyway, I feel like you care about Nana too. So, it would be just as weird for you to sort these things."

I thought about it and said: "Maybe. But to me she was a cool old bird that I liked to talk to whenever she came around. She's actually your family. Somehow, I think that trumps my friendship with her. But still, let me know if you want my help."

I kissed his neck and slipped away to go finish pulling down the rest of the things that we'd decided to bring down from the attic. The croquet set had been a given. The red ball was finally staying put in the caddy now that it was parked downstairs. At least for now anyway. Milo planned to make us all play this summer after the baby came.

Ian and I had just finished in the attic and were headed down for a beer when I heard Tom and Milo squealing with laughter. I went and popped my head into our room to see what was so funny.

"Oh, Rafe! Look what I found!" Milo was holding up an old skeleton key. "It's the key to the attic!"

"What's so funny about that? I mean it's cool and all that you found it, but I don't get why it's funny." I looked at them curiously until Tom came dancing across the room with a big pink vibrator. He waved it over his head like a lasso while dancing around in a circle and slapping his own ass. I rolled my eyes, until Milo spoke through his giggles.

"The key was in a wooden box with that thing." I looked at in horror, trying to reconcile it with the sweet little old lady that I'd met.

I turned to Ian and said: "Let's go get those beers." I heard the omegas giggle harder as I made tracks for the stairs without looking back.

CHAPTER 18

MILO

SOMETIME NEAR THE END OF MAY

I turned to Kent and Tom after we'd closed the shop for the last time before I took my paternity leave. Honestly, I was rarely there the past few months anyway. Between my swollen ankles and sore back, it was a wonder that I ever left the house.

"Now remember, Tom. Kent is the candy-maker. Stay out of his kitchen. No going in there and bugging him when you're bored like you've always done to me."

I'd found out around Valentine's Day that Kent was actually really good at making candy. He did well working alone and followed my recipes to perfection. It turned out that all Kent had needed was to find the slot that he fit in best. He'd graduated high school last week and was now available to take my place and work full-time.

Tom rolled his eyes but nodded in agreement. Tom was

my full-time employee now as well. He'd quit The Glazed Bun after I'd offered to make him the manager of Sweet Ballz. We were busy enough that we had a couple high school kids coming in part-time. Tom was amazing at organization and was actually running a tight ship.

Tom held my arm and helped me down the step to the parking lot. "Easy now, Milo. Tom's got you. Now, is Milo sure that Tom can't tempt Milo into poking into the baby boutique for a minute? There's a new display of the cutest little onesies in the window. Tom needs to check them out."

I grinned as Tom helped me into the passenger seat of his car. I wasn't driving these days. Partially because Rafe worried since I was so close to my due-date, but mostly because I had a hard time wedging my big gut behind the wheel.

"I would, Tom. But I'm so hungry!" Tom looked at me with a knowing smirk. All I did lately was eat. I'd finish a meal and then go looking for a snack. Growing a baby was hungry work apparently.

Tom backed out of the parking spot and headed toward my place. "Does Rafe have dinner ready for Milo? Because Milo is too fat to cook."

I glared over at his grinning face. "Watch it with the fat jokes, Tommy-boy. Just wait. Someday you'll be the one that's as big as a house and I'll be ready with payback."

Tom shuddered with horror. "Gawd, no! Tom will be a wonderful uncle, but Tom has no plans of birthing babies. Nope. Not happening, Milo."

"What does Ian think about that, Tom?" I asked curiously, because I really didn't know what went on between those two. They were hot and cold with each other but didn't seem to have any firm understanding or commitment between them.

Tom shrugged carelessly. "If Ian wants babies, Ian is welcome to carry them himself or find another omega. Tom gets bored of Ian sometimes anyway."

I looked at the brittle smile on his face and wondered if Tom was bluffing. And if so, how much? Did he want Ian still? Did he really not want children? Who knew with Tom. Right now, I was too busy having my own baby to worry about whether Tom wanted any of his own. I'd circle back once I was myself again.

"Tom, you'd let me know if you weren't okay though, right?" I asked quietly.

"Do not worry, Milo. Tom is fine." He flashed a quick smile at me that didn't quite reach his eyes. Then he sighed softly. "Tom doesn't know what Tom wants right now, Milo. That's the truth of it. And Ian is all party, all the time. But Tom is starting to think that maybe there is more out there. Watching Milo all cozied up with Rafe has made Tom think about the future more."

I reached over and squeezed his thigh. "Well, you know

I'm always around if you want to talk. And there's like a billion spare rooms in our house if you want to come stay for awhile. Especially after the baby comes. I want you to know that my door is always open to you. You're my family, Tommy-boy."

Tom nodded abruptly, his green eyes suspiciously bright. "Well, as much as Tom appreciates the sweet offer from Milo, Tom must decline to staying in a haunted house." We both giggled at that and the weird tension between us dissipated.

Rafe was waiting outside when we pulled in the drive. "Oh, my Gawd! Tom! Do you people realize that I'm pregnant, not an invalid? Seriously!"

Tom snorted as he put the car into park. "Sorry, Milo. When the gut enters a room before the omega, people tend to worry."

I glared over at him as Rafe opened my door. Tom snickered and waved gaily at Rafe. "Milo is all Rafe's now. Watch out for the grumpy omega. It's been a long day."

Rafe helped me out of the car. I turned back to look at Tom with a pout. "Aren't you coming in? I thought maybe you'd join us for dinner."

Tom smiled and shook his head. "Sorry, Milo love. Tom has plans at the big-O tonight."

Rafe said innocently: "Oh, say hey to Ian then. I haven't been able to get in touch with him all week."

Tom snorted and said quietly: "Join the club. Tom hasn't spoken to Ian either."

Rafe looked surprised but stepped back from the car. I blew a kiss at Tom. "Be good tonight, Tommy-boy. Call us if you need a ride or someone to bring bail money."

Tom grinned and nodded as I shut the door. He backed out and was gone before I even made it to the front door. Rafe asked: "Do I want to know?"

I shrugged. "I've tried to ask, and I'm not getting much either. I think the two of them are on the outs again."

Rafe said quietly: "Ian's got commitment issues. If things get too serious, he's the first one to leave. Every damn time. If I hear anything, I'll let you know. I know you don't want Tom to get hurt." I nodded my agreement and bit back a sigh.

"Well, Tom is just as bad. So those two together are either a disaster waiting to happen or the best thing that ever happened to either of them." I sighed and rubbed at my sore back with a fist. "I guess we'll just watch from the sidelines and see how it plays out."

"Baby, is your back bothering you again?" Rafe asked after he'd helped me get settled on the couch.

I nodded. "It's really bad today. It comes and goes. But

nothing that I can't live with for our baby." I smiled up at him. "Is it too soon to ask what's for dinner?"

Rafe barked out a laugh. "I had Luigi's deliver a large pepperoni and pineapple pizza right before you got here."

My eyes lit up when he mentioned my favorite pizza. "Okay, okay. Sit tight, I'll be right back with it, babe." Rafe left to get the pizza while I leaned back and plopped my feet onto the coffee table with a happy groan of contentment.

"Oh, man. I'm so happy to finally be in bed!" I moaned as Rafe massaged my back while I laid on my side. "Ooh, yeah, right there."

Rafe's massaging hands moved down to squeeze my butt while he moved closer and kissed the nape of my neck. "You know what, baby? Your massage moans sound remarkably similar to your sexy-time moans." His hand slipped around to grip my already hard dick. "Does massage turn my man on?"

"Mmhmm." I moaned, pushing into his grip. I looked back over my shoulder. "I'm not saying no, you know."

Rafe chuckled and nipped at my earlobe. "Baby? I'd be surprised if you were." I grinned, knowing as well as Rafe did how horny that pregnancy had made me. I pushed my butt up against his hard cock, giving a little wiggle of invitation.

"Oh, it's like that, huh? Someone looking for a little more than a massage?" His hand was working my dick now, stroking me with a firm grip while he nibbled at my ear. The combination of his warm breath on my skin and the tickle of his goatee had me squirming for more.

"Baby?" I moaned as my head rolled back against his. "Get the lube."

Rafe chuckled and released me long enough to retrieve the lube from his nightstand drawer. "How will it be the most comfortable for you, baby? Want to ride me or spoon?" Our options were limited now, due to the sheer size of my baby belly and my recent back pain.

"Spoon me, hon. I'm just gonna lie here like a lazy ass and let you have your way with me, okay?" I bent my knee and shifted to give him easier access.

His lubed finger slipped up inside my hole. I shivered with delight as a second went in to join the first. Rafe kissed along my neck and shoulders while his fingers worked my hole. He hit that magical little bundle of nerves with both fingers at once.

"Rafe!" I groaned as he rubbed me almost to completion right there. "I'm good, babe. Fill me now. Enough teasing."

Rafe shifted down a little and lifted my leg up with a firm grip on my thigh. He pushed the head of his cock against my tight ring of muscle and slowly eased inside. His thumb stroked the side of my thigh where he held it. He slowly pushed in and then slid out of my love tunnel. Pushing back with my hips, I rocked against him desperately.

Reading my cues, Rafe pushed in harder on the next thrust. He lifted my arm with his free hand and leaned over my chest to get at my nipple. My balls were so tight, I was right at the edge already. My vision blurred as lightening streaked through my body. Rafe bit down on my nipple as he thrust faster. Harder. Deeper. His fat cock brushed up against that magical little nerve bundle with each rock of his hips.

Pulling off my nipple, he nuzzled my armpit while never losing rhythm. He moved around my arm to get to my face. Plunging his tongue into my mouth, Rafe kissed me hard and rough. His hips were pounding against me now.

With a loud groan, I threw my head back as ropes of cum suddenly shot across the bed in front of me. I clenched all my muscles as I came. I felt his cock swell inside of me as my channel hugged him when I clenched up. Rafe growled into my mouth as his hips jerked a few times then slowed.

He broke our kiss and licked a stripe down my neck before planting a kiss on my shoulder. I could feel the heat of his release inside me as I lay panting against him. He lowered my leg and carefully pulled out. While I lay recovering from our passion, Rafe got up from the bed.

He went into the bathroom, only to return a moment later with a wet towel. He lovingly cleaned me up, then kissed the swell of my stomach before carrying the towel back into the bathroom. Seconds later he was crawling back into bed and snuggling up behind me.

His arm came around my waist, his hand resting on my stomach protectively. "Good night, Milo. I love you, my little pumpkin spiced omega." He whispered this against my ear.

I smiled sleepily and murmured: "I love you too, Rafe. So much more than I can ever say. Good night, hon." Safe in his arms, I drifted off to sleep.

I woke up a few hours later. My back was clenched into a tight spasm while a white-hot pain pierced my gut. I was drenched in sweat, and unable to move. I screamed out as the pain deepened.

Rafe jerked awake behind me, his head lifting as spoke drowsily. "Milo? What's wrong, baby?"

"I don't know. It hurts! Make it stop, Rafe! Oh, fuuuuck!" Rafe's hand came down against my belly as I writhed in agony.

"I'm calling 911, I think these are contractions. Your gut is hard and tight. I don't like the way your covered in sweat either. Shit, baby. Hold on!"

Rafe sat up and grabbed his cell off the nightstand. I barely understood him as he spoke into the phone, the pain was too fucking intense. After that, everything was a blur.

CHAPTER 19
RAFE

I stared at the doctor in dismay, unable to make sense of the words that he was saying. Luckily, Tom came flying up right then. Thank fuck that I'd had the presence of mind to call him as I'd anxiously followed the ambulance to the hospital.

"What's wrong with Milo?" Tom cut right to the chase. The doctor looked at me, but Tom snapped his fingers abruptly to get his attention. "I'm Milo's brother. It's okay to talk to me, tell him Rafe." I nodded weakly at Tom's order, relieved to have the bossy little omega there to help take charge.

"I was just explaining to Mr. Smythe that your brother has placental abruption. That happens when the plac-"

"Forget all that. I'll research it later," Tom interrupted. "Tell us what you're going to do about it."

"Oh, that's simple." The doctor said with obvious relief.

"We're going to give Milo a C-section." He looked from Tom to me. "One of you can be in the room, if you'd like. We're preparing him now." He pointed to the nursing station. "Just go have one of the nurses help you get changed and we'll see you in there."

I looked at Tom, at a loss as to what I was supposed to do. Tom looked at me and pulled himself up into my face. I pushed back the urge to cower from the bossy little twink as he glared up into my eyes.

"Listen here, Rafe. I know you're scared shitless right now. And that's okay. I am too. But you know what? Fuck. That. You are going to alpha the fuck up and put it aside. Break down all you want later when it's done. But now? Now you're going to go in there. You're going to hold Milo's hand, stroke his head, tell him he's beautiful and all that other shit that he needs to hear from you right now. I would do it, but I'm not the one that he needs in there. You are. Are you with me? Can you do this for Milo?"

I nodded hesitantly, slowly coming back to myself as I pushed the fear aside. "Good. Now let's go see a nurse about some scrubs."

Tom took charge with the nurses, charming them into doing his bidding. Before I knew it, I was wearing a paper gown and scrub pants over my clothes. I had a mask over the lower half of my face and was being led into the room where they had Milo.

As soon as I saw him, laid out on the table with a curtain blocking his lower half from view, I rushed over. I ignored the sight of them preparing to slice into his abdomen, and instead I reached for his hand. I looked into his eyes, so clouded by pain and fear. All at once, my own fears vanished and were replaced by a primal need to protect and comfort my mate.

I leaned over and touched my forehead to his. "It's okay, baby. I know that this isn't the birth plan that we expected. But you know what? Shit happens, right? Now you just get to lay here and relax while the doctor delivers the baby. Doesn't that sound better than fifteen hours of labor?"

I got a smile out of him. A weak smile, but a smile nonetheless. Encouraged, I kept talking. "Tom is out there, taking charge as usual. I think he's tripping though. He had an entire conversation with me and the doctor and didn't slip into third person once."

Milo smiled at that and said in a hoarse voice: "Wow, that means he is really freaking out then."

I nodded. "So, any last-minute bets on what gender we're getting?" Milo rolled his eyes and squeezed my hand. He'd refused to find out the gender, insisting that he wanted it to be a surprise. I'd tried to argue that the baby was a surprise in and of itself, but he didn't back down.

"I don't have a preference," Milo rasped. "I just want a

healthy baby. Although I won't hate if our baby has your emerald green eyes."

Before I had a chance to respond, a squawking cry filled the room. My eyes teared up as the doctor held up a gunk covered baby boy. "Congratulations, gentleman! It's a boy!" He handed the baby to a nurse, who whisked him off to clean him up.

Milo and I watched as the nurses fussed over our son across the room, while the doctor finished doing whatever he was doing on the other side of the curtain. I looked down at Milo. "Does it hurt, babe? Did you feel anything?"

"No, it's totally weird." Milo rasped in his hoarse voice. "I'm completely numb from the waist down, but I can feel them tugging at me. If that makes sense?"

I nodded. "Well, considering what they're doing, I bet you do feel some tugging. I just hope it doesn't hurt too bad when the drugs wear off."

Milo smiled softly. "It doesn't matter. It's all worth it for him. Besides, nothing can hurt as much as that god-awful lancing pain that I had when I woke up tonight."

I nodded with complete understanding. The nurse brought the baby over then and helped me figure out how to hold him properly. She smiled regretfully at Milo. "I'm sorry, hon. You can't hold him just yet. But don't worry, you'll have sore arms from lugging this little prince around soon enough!"

Milo nodded and craned his head to see our son. I dipped sideways and tilted my arm so that he could see our baby too. Milo gasped with pleasure as he drank him in. "Look at that little rosebud mouth and button nose, Rafe! Have you ever seen anything more adorable than him in your entire life?"

I smirked at Milo and said: "Is that a trick question, baby?"

Milo chuckled and said: "No. I'm being serious. Besides, I'm the cute one and he's the adorable one. See? Easy peasy."

We cooed over our son until they said that Milo needed to go to recovery. The nurses took the baby to the nursery, and I went out to tell Tom the good news.

As soon as I walked out of the room and lowered my mask, Tom was up in my face. He bounced up on the balls of his feet excitedly and said: "Well? Tell Tom! What is going on in there?"

I grinned proudly and said: "It's a boy! Come on, they took him to the nursery, but we can see him through the window they said. Milo will be in recovery for a couple of hours before he gets moved to a room."

Tom threw himself at me. I caught him and gave him a firm hug. I could feel the relief from him as he hugged me back. As he pulled away, I caught his arm and said in a serious voice: "Tom. Thank you for jerking me back to reality earlier. And for always being there for both of us."

Tom blushed and said: "It's no problem. Like Tom said, Milo is Tom's brother. And now Tom has a nephew to spoil!" He gave a sideways glance and added: "Tom supposes if pressed that Rafe is Tom's brother now as well."

I grinned and put my arm over his shoulder as I led him to the nursery. "Damn straight I am! Are you kidding me? You're the annoying little brother that I never knew I wanted. Beats the shit out of the one I'm related to by blood. If you ever meet him, you'll probably end up bitch slapping him."

Tom snorted, and I laughed. "No, seriously. My kid brother is a spoiled little shit. He's off in Europe somewhere with my mom. Or at least they were the last I heard from them. Who knows. It's not like they stay in contact with me."

Tom looked at me and said: "That sucks, Rafe. Family isn't supposed to be that way. Why does Rafe's family act like that?"

I shrugged and replied: "Best guess? I don't act rich enough for them. They're ashamed of me because I don't waste my life getting drunk and eating caviar."

Tom shook his head. "Damn. Well, Rafe has Tom and Milo now." He grinned. "And Tom's nephew! Never forget the nephew!"

CHAPTER 20

MILO

OCTOBER

I looked at Tom. "What did they look like? Do they look like Rafe?"

He shrugged. "Like a couple of rich assholes. Tom doesn't understand how Rafe came from the same family tree as those douche-canoes out there."

"And what about Arthur? Is he okay? They're not trying to handle him too much are they? I mean, I know he's their family too. But, shit. I mean, they didn't even come when he was born!" I looked in the full-length mirror at the line of my jacket while Tom adjusted my tie.

"Artie is fine. Kent is holding Artie. That young alpha will protect young Artie. Milo just needs to relax and get through the ceremony."

I nodded. It had been a long time coming, but Rafe and I were finally getting married today. Actually, in a few minutes. I was nervous. Not because I was marrying Rafe, but because his mother and brother had decided to grace us with their presence at the last minute. They'd shown up a few minutes ago, and Tom had immediately come to warn me.

"And Rafe? Rafe knows?" I asked Tom urgently, suddenly worried that the arrival of his family would ruin our wedding day for my alpha.

Tom sighed. "Milo. Stop worrying. Rafe is the one that let the assholes in the door. Rafe seemed fine, Artie is fine, and Milo needs to take a gigantic chill pill."

I smiled and leaned into my friend for a hug. "Thanks, Tom. Thanks for always being there for me, no matter what. Now, let's go get me married. What do you say?"

Tom turned and held out a stiff elbow. "Tom says that it's about fucking time."

I was still giggling as Tom and I walked down the stairs and into the ballroom together. Rafe and Ian were waiting at the front of the room. They stood on the right side of the altar area as it faced the gathered guests. They were in front of the gorgeous lilac covered trellis that Rafe had insisted on us having. The rented chairs were sheathed in floor length covers of white damask and tied off with big silver bows.

Tom and I walked down the silver aisle runner side by side. My eyes never left Rafe's as I headed toward my happily ever after. When we reached the trellis, Tom stepped off to the left as I went forward to join hands with Rafe.

The attendant spoke of love and commitment, which I already felt every time that I looked into my beloved's eyes. This ceremony was just a formality. Our forever had begun a year ago, inside of a tacky club with glittery go-go boys in cages. I heard Artie making noise and glanced over at the front row where Kent held him carefully on his lap. I smiled. Kent really was a good kid. And my son really was the most adorable thing in the entire universe.

Soon enough, we were exchanging vows. We'd opted to say our own vows, with a little of the traditional alpha/omega vows mixed in. We'd written them separately with neither of us knowing what the other was going to say. I looked at Rafe when the attendant told me it was time.

"Rafe. I never thought that I would find an alpha like you. Even the alphas in my favorite books couldn't hold a candle to the reality that is you. You're the reason that I smile when I wake up in the morning, and why I thank God when I fall asleep at night. You're my mate, my alpha, the father of my child, and now my husband. I love you, Rafe. And I vow to love you, honor you, and stay by your side through bad haircuts, foul moods, and horrible reviews."

Rafe grinned at me, his eyes wet with unshed tears as he said his vow to me.

"Milo. When I found you, I thought that I was the luckiest man alive. When you forgave me for being an alpha-hole, I knew that I was the luckiest man alive. You're the song in my heart, the light in my darkness, and the beat in my heart. You're my mate, my omega, the father of my child, and now my husband. I love you, Milo. I will always love you, both in this life and the next. I vow to love you, honor you, and stay by your side through haunted houses, dead relatives, and random appearances of red croquet balls."

The attendant looked at us with a curious smile, and said: "Milo and Rafe, I now pronounce you to be husbands, and mates. Long may you live and love in peace my friends." Rafe was already pulling me into his arms when the attendant continued: "Rafe, you may now kiss your omega."

Our friends and family cheered as Rafe pulled me into his arms for a long kiss. When we pulled away and turned to face our guests, the attendant proclaimed loudly: "Ladies and Gentlemen, may I present Mr. and Mr. Smythe".

Right as he said that, all the lights in the house began to flicker and the clear sound of jazz music filled the air. Rafe smiled and leaned over to hug me while he whispered in my ear: "I'm pretty sure that's your family giving their approval."

The strong smell of lilacs filled the air as he spoke. I glanced back at the trellis, but Rafe whispered: "Tell yourself whatever you need to hear to sleep at night, but the flowers on the trellis are silk, baby."

I gasped as I looked over my husband's shoulder. Over at the edge of the room, I clearly saw my dad, my father, and my dear Nana standing there smiling at me. I blinked my eyes and turned to tell Rafe. But when I looked back, they were gone.

Rafe led me over to take Artie from Kent. He lifted our son up onto his shoulder and we walked down the silver runner together as a family. As we walked through the doorway, I noticed the red croquet ball sitting on the floor at the foot of the stairs.

I pointed it out to Rafe. He looked over at it fondly and then back at me. "Milo? You're my little red ball, baby. Don't ever forget that." I smiled and leaned into my husband. My very own living red ball.

Fin

AUTHOR'S NOTE

I would like to give some special thanks with more appreciation than I could ever express to my fabulous Glam-Squad of Beta Readers! This book wouldn't be the same without your input. I am very fortunate to have the support of faithful reader friends like each of you.

-Susi

Thank you for reading *Pumpkin Spiced Omega*. If you've enjoyed this book, please leave a review recommending this story to other readers. Make sure to mention your favorite part; I always look forward to reading reviews! If you'd like to know who gets a happy ending next in The Hollydale Omegas, keep reading for a sneak preview of *Cinnamon Spiced Omega*.

CHAPTER 21

CHRISTIAN

"It's the head gasket, sir. I'm going to need another day before your car will be ready." I was looking over my schedule, while I balanced the phone on my ear.

The man's irate voice let out a stream of profanities before finally sighing and asking: "I assume this means that the higher estimate you quoted is the one I'm looking at now."

Returning my focus to the matter at hand, I agreed and quoted the new estimate. I finished our conversation and hung up the phone. It was always a bitch to give people bad news about their cars, but at least I could usually fix the problem. Eventually.

I took a drink of coffee, irritated to notice that it had gone cold. After I quickly updated the file for the repair that had just been authorized, I stood and went back out to the garage. An old Kansas tune was blasting in the cavernous space, joining the cacophony of the other sounds that filled my workday.

The clamor of a metal tool hitting the cement floor when Scott dropped a wrench over by Mr. Tso's Prius, the impact gun Neal was currently using to remove the lug nuts from Mrs. Peterman's Buick, the revving engine coming from '78 Camaro where Tim was checking the carburetor: these were the sounds of my world.

Tim poked his head around the hood, wiping his hands on the shop rag that hung from the pocket of his navy coveralls. "Hey, boss man. Are we a go on the Dodge? I already talked to Dennis over at the machine shop, they can fit us in first thing tomorrow for the head resurfacing. I told him I'd drop it off by the end of the day if you gave the thumbs up."

"Sounds good, Tim. Both thumbs way up, we're definitely a go. He wasn't thrilled, but can't say I blame him. He's already sunk a lot into that old beater."

"True. But once he gets past all this, it's gonna be a good, solid ride for his kid. Hell, it's gonna be too much car for the kid if you ask me." Tim smirked at the old muscle car parked over in bay five. "With a good restoration job and a complete overhaul on the engine, that car would be my baby. I'd never need to get laid again. That car would be enough to do it for me."

Chuckling, I shook my head. "Yeah, well, instead it will be doing it for a teen-aged alpha. I don't know how much his dad plans to fix it up, but he did mention it's getting painted next week."

Tim shook his head and turned back to the Camaro. "Well, shit. That kid won't be sitting home on Friday nights. He's pretty much guaranteed to get all the action he wants if they do even a half decent job painting it. Those little omegas will go nuts over him."

"I imagine they already are, since he's on the football team. Oh, well. Forget the kid. Tell me some good news about this Camaro. I need to call the owner for an update. He's already left two messages this morning."

"Sure thing, Chris. It's not as bad as we'd expected. Come on over, let me walk you through it."

After he filled me in, I went back to the office to call the customer. The rest of the morning flew by, one car or customer at a time. At lunch time, I dragged myself out of the office and decided to go check in on my kid brother over at Sweet Ballz where he'd worked since high school.

I'd opened Greasy Fingers Garage here in Hollydale about five years ago. I had moved home to take care of my kid brother after our omega dad died. Neither of us knew our alpha fathers. It had always just been the three of us. The three amigos. The three musketeers. It had been a ballsy move to open my own business with my share of the meager life insurance our dad had left for us, especially for a kid just barely old enough to drink.

I had needed the income to take care of my brother, and mechanics was what I knew. When I saw that the town had no decent garage, it had seemed like a no-brainer. Luckily, it had paid off. Now I had a good staff and a steady stream of customers. My brother had been able to finish high school and never needed to worry about having a roof over his head.

Kent was six years younger than me. He was twenty now, but still so young in so many ways. His job at the candy shop was a perfect fit for him. My dad would've loved to know that his younger alpha son made a living making candy. It was so different from the career paths that most alphas took. Kent was a gentler alpha though. He was a sweet kid, with none of the normal alpha characteristics, at least not so far. Maybe he just hadn't come in to his own yet.

I headed out the backdoor of the garage, ducking through the alley that separated my garage from the backside of the row of shops where Sweet Ballz was located. As I passed the row of dumpsters that served the different businesses, an old man stepped out from between two of them.

Jumping back, I willed myself to calm down and breathe. The old dude looked harmless enough but his sudden appearance had scared the shit out of me. He was shorter than me, his head about level with my shoulder. The sunlight sparkled against his shiny bald head, highlighting the wispy white hairs that grew in sparse little patches around the sides and back of his head.

He was about two days past shaving, with a grizzled white stubble covering his wrinkled jaw. I looked into his surprisingly sharp blue eyes that twinkled merrily. The old guy was grinning like a loon, his yellowed teeth flashing.

"Whoa, there! You kids are always in hurry. Almost stopped my heart, you coming up like that."

I grinned back at him. "I think you have that back-wards, sir. I'm pretty sure that I'm the one who almost had the heart attack with the way that you jumped out at me."

He chuckled with the breathy rasp of a lifetime smoker. "Sorry, kid. And the name's Otis, no need to bother with that sir shit. What are you doing back here anyway, kid?" Otis dug around in the pocket of his crackled leather jacket, looking for something. No old man cardigans for this guy, he even wore his khakis at his natural waist level, instead of up to his armpits like most old timers.

"Okay, Otis. I'm Chris. I own the shop back there," I pointed a thumb over my shoulder in the direction of my shop. I wasn't entirely sure why I'd extended the conversation, but I continued. “I haven’t seen you around here before, Otis. Are you new in town?”

Otis finally found what he was looking for as he triumphantly pulled a partially smoked cigar out of his pocket. He lit it and gave a few satisfied puffs before answering me. I took a polite step to the side, hoping to get out of the path of his smoke.

“Not new, no. Just don’t get around as much as I used to, I suppose.” He spoke around the fat cigar that was now nestled in the corner of his mouth. He eyes glinted with humor, as though laughing at a private joke.

“Oh, I see. Well, it was nice to meet you, Otis. I’m actually headed over to have lunch with my kid brother. Can I bring you anything? Or would you like to join us?” Again, I had no idea why I’d offered that, but the satisfied gleam in his eye told me that it had been the right thing to say.

“Ha! I knew you were a good kid. I always was a good judge of character. Nah, kid. I’m good. I’ll be around for awhile, so we’ll see each other again. Count on it.”

It felt like I was being dismissed, so I took the hint. “Alright, Otis. Well, it was nice to meet you. I’m right over there in the Greasy Fingers Garage if you ever need to find me. I’d better get going before I run out of time for lunch.”

With a grin and a wave, I hurried on down the alley and ducked into the backdoor of the kitchen where

Kent would be busy rolling balls or melting chocolate. Today he was rolling doughy balls, with the help of the store manager, Tom.

Tom looked up as I came in the door. As I pulled it shut behind me, he gave me the once over and pointed to the sink. "As much as Tom loves a grease covered alpha, Christian must wash up first."

I grinned. "Well, I washed my hands before I came over, but no problem. This is a kitchen, I get it. Do you want me to take off the coveralls or put on an apron?"

Tom fanned his face. "What does Christian have on under those coveralls? Do not disappoint Tom, alpha."

I slowly lowered my zipper with a teasing grin, enjoying the way the bossy little omega eyed me as I removed them to reveal a tight-fitting tank top and running shorts. I laid them on the counter by the back-door with a shrug. "What? It gets hot under those but I don't wear them when Kent and I go to lunch. So, yeah. Light clothes underneath."

Kent's head came up then. He looked over at the clock and back down at the table in front of him, before turning to look at me with wide eyes. "I'm sorry, Chun! I lost track of time. There's no way I can leave right now. This order needs to get done by five."

I smiled at the childhood nickname Kent insisted on calling me. When he was little, he couldn't say Christ-ian. Instead, it had come out as 'Chun' and had stuck within our family ever since. "It's okay, Kent. I'll be happy to run and grab us all sandwiches from next door if you want?"

Tom gave me another slow elevator eye treatment. "Tom will call in an order. Christian can help Kent play with his balls."

He and I both snickered. Seriously, when Kent's boss had named this place he obviously hadn't been thinking about all the ball jokes that would just roll off the tongue. Even the name. Sweet Ballz? It was epic. I grinned at Tom and went over to take his place as he got up to go order our usual from the Sub Shoppe next door. Seriously. It was named Sub Shoppe. This town and its names. That's why I'd gone for the tongue in cheek name Greasy Fingers when I'd named my garage. Not only did I get to laugh at the pun, I fit right in with the rest of the businesses.

Kent was barely noticing me as he deftly rolled the little balls of dough and lined them up on the paper covered trays that were arranged in the center of the large metal island where we were working. I began rolling the balls, making sure they were the same size as the others or Kent would freak out on me. I'd made that mistake before.

"Hey, Kent. What are these? They smell interesting. Almost like apple pie."

Kent's head came up, his eyes lit with excitement. "I

know! This is for a special fall party at the apple orchard. They're celebrating the new cider recipe and asked me to use the cider in a hands-free dessert. This is a basic cookie dough, done with the apple cider and little bits of apple. Once we're done rolling them, I'll bake them. After they're cool, I'm dipping them in cinnamon infused white chocolate."

I shook my head, amazed at his creativity. "And you came up with this recipe yourself?"

Kent shrugged. "Milo and I were spit-balling ideas after the order came in. I suggested this idea. We tried a few different recipes until we ended up with this one. They're actually really good. It's like a mix of a snicker-doodle and apple pie, if I had to describe it. They will be more like a cookie ball then a candy ball, but that's fine. We're calling them Cider Ballz."

My stomach growled then, making us both laugh. "Can I just ask you to save me a few? I really need to try these. You know how much I love cinnamon. And apples. Damn, Kent. These are my dessert version of a wet dream."

As if my words had conjured him, Tom popped through the swinging door from the main shop right then. He held a bag of sandwiches in the crook of his arm, and a big grin on his face. "Oooh. Tom arrived just in time. Christian needs to tell Tom more about these wet dreams."

I tossed him a wink and went back to rolling balls. I figured we'd be done in about five minutes and then I could dig into the food Tom held. "Is there more dough to roll, Kent? Or will we be done after this last bit?"

Kent shook his head. "No, this is the last of it. As soon as we get them all done, I'll slip the first batch into the oven and we can eat."

Tom slid onto the stool beside me and waited for us to finish while he scrolled on his phone. I spent another half hour with them. As soon as I finished eating, I reluctantly slid my coveralls back on so I could head back to work. As pleasant as these little breaks with my brother were, I had a business to run. I said good-bye to Tom and reminded Kent to bring some of those amazing Cider Ballz home with him tonight.

While I was walking back down the alley, I thought back to my earlier meeting with the interesting old guy. It didn't surprise me that Otis was long gone. I just wondered if I'd ever see him again, and what his story was anyway. When I passed the spot where I'd met him, a large feather caught my eye. I bent down and picked it up.

It was a pristine white quill feather with golden edges. The feather was long and wide. It looked just like the ones used for, well, feather pens. I held it up, admiring its beauty. There was no way this came from a bird. It had to have blown here from someone who used it for crafts or designs of some sort. It was too beautiful to be found in nature.

I was still holding it when I walked into my office. I laid it on the shelf where I kept photos of my family from when we were younger. My dad would've loved this feather. Fanciful bits of fluff had been his thing. Smiling, I gave it one last glance and went back to work. I had customers to deal with, parts to order, and a garage full of cars waiting to be fixed.

What did you think? Want to know what happens next? You can buy *Cinnamon Spiced Omega* right now—just navigate to the link below.

Cinnamon Spiced Omega: Book 2
https://amazon.com/dp/B076HXC945

Cupid always gives you a second chance...

Join my mailing list and get your FREE copy of Strawberry Spiced Omega

https://dl.bookfunnel.com/io4ia6hgz8

Twitter:

https://twitter.com/SusiHawkeAuthor

Facebook:

https://www.facebook.com/SusiHawkeAuthor

ALSO BY SUSI HAWKE

Northern Lodge Pack Series

Omega Stolen: Book 1

Omega Remembered: Book 2

Omega Healed: Book 3

Omega Shared: Book 4

Omega Matured: Book 5

Omega Accepted: Book 6

Omega Grown: Book 7

Northern Pines Den Series

Alpha's Heart: Book 1

Alpha's Mates: Book 2

Alpha's Strength: Book 3

Alpha's Wolf: Book 4

Alpha's Redemption: Book 5

Alpha's Solstice: Book 6

Blood Legacy Chronicles

Alpha's Dream: Book 1

Omega Found: Book 2

Omega's Destiny: Book 3

Alpha's Dom: Book 4

Alpha's Charm: Book 5

Omega's Mark: Book 6

Alpha's Seal: Book 7

The Hollydale Omegas

Pumpkin Spiced Omega: Book 1

Cinnamon Spiced Omega: Book 2

Peppermint Spiced Omega: Book 3

Champagne Spiced Omega: Book 4

Chocolate Spiced Omega: Book 5

Shamrock Spiced Omega: Book 6

Marshmallow Spiced Omega: Book 7

Three Hearts Collection

(with Harper B. Cole)

The Surrogate Omega: Book 1

The Divorced Omega: Book 2

Waking the Dragons

(with Piper Scott)

Alpha Awakened: Book 1

Alpha Ablaze: Book 2

Alpha Deceived: Book 3

Alpha Victorious: Book 4

Team A.L.P.H.A.

(with Crista Crown)

Grabbed: Book 1

Taken: Book 2

MacIntosh Meadows

The Alpha's Widower: Book 1

The Omega's Dance: Book 2

Made in the USA
Lexington, KY
24 July 2019